C0-DLY-934

McLEAN INVESTIGATES
George Goodchild

Connoisseurs of the detective story have long appreciated the crisp, economical style of George Goodchild and the ingenuity of his plots. Here, for his many admirers are sixteen typical examples of his art showing his inimitable creation — Inspector McLean of the Yard — at his all-time best.

Also by
GEORGE GOODCHILD
in this series
INSPECTOR McLEAN'S CASEBOOK
McLEAN SOLVES IT
CALL McLEAN

GEORGE GOODCHILD

McLean Investigates

LONDON
WHITE LION PUBLISHERS LIMITED

George Goodchild
McLEAN INVESTIGATES

© Copyright, George Goodchild, 1930

First published in the United Kingdom by
Hodder and Stoughton, 1930

First published in this White Lion edition, 1972

SBN 85617 681 8

Published by
White Lion Publishers Limited,
91/93 Baker Street,
London W1M 1FA
and printed in Spain
by Euredit

McLEAN INVESTIGATES

SHORTLY after nine o'clock on a perfect September evening, John Tillings walked from the village inn at Redwood in Sussex to his home which lay a mile along a deserted country lane. He was a man of about forty years of age, and it was his custom to spend an hour each evening at the inn, where he usually managed to find someone to engage in a combat at dominoes. By vocation he was a small-holder, a man of some education, and a peaceful and law-abiding citizen.

At half-past nine a lad stumbled over the body of Tillings. The clothes were covered with blood, and there was a terrible wound over the left temple. The village constable was brought, and Tillings was conveyed to his home—there being no hospital within ten miles. Twenty hours passed before he recovered consciousness, and another twenty-four before he was able to make a statement to the police. There wasn't much to tell. He had seen a light approaching him, and soon discerned a bicycle being pushed by a man, who appeared to be powerfully built. The oncomer stopped within a yard of him and inquired if he were far from the village. Tillings was replying when the left arm of the man—previously hidden behind his back—dealt him a smashing blow. The rest was a blank.

He did not think he could describe the face with any accuracy, for the light shed by the bicycle lamp was not good, and the owner of it was in the shadow all the time. He thought the suit of his assailant was of a brown shade—but was not sure. Motive? He could not think of one. He had no enemies, and the money he had in his pocket was intact—also his watch. It was later that he discovered his eye-glasses were missing.

A search for these was made on the spot of the brutal attack, but without success. It was concluded that they must have fallen from his nose, and been picked up by a pedestrian who had failed to hand them over to the police. The whole thing remained wrapped in mystery, and was the talk of the village for some time.

A month passed, and during this period there were strange sequels to the Redwood affair. From various parts of Sussex came reports of attacks of a similar nature. In every case the culprit was a man with a bicycle—now proved to be painted green. The descriptions of the man varied, but all the victims agreed he was big and clean-shaven. In some cases he approached them from behind—

sometimes from the front. In one instance the victim was a girl, and as a result the public became incensed.

At Scotland Yard, McLean was wading through a pile of reports dealing with the matter. On the other side of the table Sergeant Brook was tabulating dates and times. Brook was displaying unusual interest, for Brook loved cases of this sort. The more subtle deeds of habitual law-breakers did not appeal to him much. His idea of a hundred-per-cent. criminal was one who battered out brains without compunction. The Man with the Green Bicycle—as the Press now termed him—was such.

" That makes nine cases—so far," mused Brook. " And all in Sussex ! "

" What period do the various times cover ? "

" The first one I have is round about eight-thirty—the last at close on eleven o'clock."

" Hm ! Now give me that large-scale map."

The two worked on the map for some time, McLean writing in the dates and times of the attacks against the vicinities in which they took place. By inscribing a circle enclosing all the places of the crimes it was seen that those which took place earlier in the evening were nearer the centre of the circle. It was rather what he expected.

" Our friend presumably leaves his home round about the same time," he said. " A systematic kind of person—possibly employed in business until a certain hour in the evening."

" What about the spectacles, sir ? In every case either spectacles or eye-glasses are missing. That can't be a coincidence ? "

" That, my dear Brook, is the motive—and that only."

" But why ? At least three of the victims carried valuables, and not a blessed thing was touched except spectacles. Queer sort of thing to go mad about ! "

" I agree. That is a little puzzling at the moment. I intend taking a trip into Sussex to-morrow. We may be away a week or more."

" You need me ? "

" Yes. If we run into the man with the green bicycle it is likely he may prove a very obstinate person."

For several days McLean and Brook moved about the Sussex coast, taking fresh statements from victims. A little more information emerged, but nothing of prime importance. On the fourth night the " spectacle-snatcher " was busy again. McLean, who had given his telephone number to all the neighbouring police-stations, was rung up and told that a man had been found in a lane near the village of Saltby—five miles away. The report had only just come in, and the village constable was now leaving.

" The car ! " said McLean.

Brook went off like a shot from a gun. In less than a quarter of an hour he and McLean were on the scene of the trouble. The village constable had just arrived, and a car was waiting to take the man away. He bore the usual head injury, and was conscious enough to gasp the details. He had been walking towards the village when a cycle overtook him. He stepped close to the hedge as the cycle swerved dangerously near to him. A big man was riding it, and had struck at him without dismounting. He had caught a glimpse of a white bar—ere it fell on his head. Then, while he was dazed, his spectacles had been wrenched off. The man had ridden on.

" Which way ? " asked McLean.

" There."

" Come on, Brook ! "

They drove the car in the direction apparently taken by the man on the bicycle, and after covering six miles without any luck, turned back and tried again in another direction. Five different branch roads were taken in all, and ultimately the search had to be abandoned.

" Blooming ghost ! " growled Brook.

" Scarcely. There is a veritable network of by-roads in the locality. Well, he seems to have got clean away again, and we have lost an excellent chance of landing him."

"Extraordinary—the spectacle business! What do you make of that, sir?"

McLean shook his head in his habitual non-communicative way. He had a theory, and meant to try it out soon, but it involved a vast amount of detail, and was less attractive than a man-hunt with a capture at the end of it. He waited in the hope of receiving another summons to the scene of an attack, but none came. The man with the green bicycle was apparently taking a rest.

Then came a piece of information which sounded promising. A village policeman got into communication with McLean. He had been looking through his "lost property" book and had found an entry of some interest. It was to the effect that a green bicycle, belonging to a workman in the village, mysteriously disappeared on the evening of August 28.

"We'll run down there," said McLean. "Cycle thefts in country villages are somewhat rare, and curiously enough the date on which this theft took place is but a few days before the first green bicycle case was reported. There may be a connection."

The village lay near the coast—within a mile of the sea. It was a delightful spot, utterly unspoiled by modern "improvements." The small collection of cob houses clustered round a beautiful Norman church, from which one could see a fine coast-line on either hand. The police station was nothing more than a room in a private house. McLean saw the sergeant in charge.

"Inspector McLean," he said. "I received your communication. Is the owner of the lost cycle available?"

"No, sir. He has left the district temporarily, but I have secured all the details from his son. The cycle was left outside the 'George and Crown' on the evening of August 28. The owner went into the inn at eight-thirty and came out at eight-forty-five. In the intervening quarter of an hour the cycle was taken. It was a Humber machine, painted green, with an oil head-lamp, but no rear light."

"Fixed gear?"

"Yes. And in place of a bell it carried a very small bulb-horn. Notice was given to me the same evening, and I have since kept a sharp look-out. But no one in the village is under suspicion. The cycle was too well known—even if we harboured a thief, which we don't."

McLean could well believe that. A policeman's job in such a delectable spot seemed to be somewhat of a sinecure. But this new information was of value, for the village was very close to the centre of the circle which he had plotted and in which area every one of the assaults had taken place.

"You know the district, Sergeant?"

"Aye. I was born here."

" Any lunatic asylums ? "

" None within five miles. There's one at Wareing—five miles along the coast; another at Dench—ten miles to the east. I believe there is a private clinic, run by a brain specialist, at Sillington. But when I knew the place it was a large country house."

" Where is Sillington ? "

" Two miles along the coast road. You follow the golf-links until you reach the river, then cross the bridge and turn inland. The house can be seen from almost anywhere. A fine place."

" Owner ? "

" I'll look it up."

He referred to a local directory and found the name. It was Dr. Charles du Park. McLean thanked him and decided to pay an immediate visit to the clinic.

§

Sillington Manor was a stately Elizabethan mansion, situated in its own park. It was surrounded by an extremely high wall—five feet of which had obviously been added quite recently, and adorned with spikes. The gate was a massive affair, and guarded by a neat lodge. There was nothing to inform a passer-by that it was a private clinic. All the brass plate, on the gate-post, bore was the name of Dr. du Park, to which was added a number of professional degrees.

McLean rang the bell, and a porter appeared and asked his business. On expressing a wish to see the doctor the porter telephoned through to the house, and McLean, on foot, was permitted to enter the drive. In the grounds he saw several men, walking and lounging. They were fairly well-dressed and well-behaved. But he noticed a tall fellow, in a not too conspicuous uniform, walking around, and keeping an observant eye on his flock.

Dr. du Park turned out to be French. But he spoke English almost perfectly, and was a quite jovial individual. When McLean proffered his card he looked astonished, but waved him into a comfortable chair and begged him to state his business.

"You have heard of 'The Man with the Green Bicycle,' doctor?"

"Certainly. One cannot help hearing of him. He is a splendid asset to the Press."

"Well, from certain information in my possession I am convinced that this man is a lunatic, and is probably sheltering in some institution such as this."

"But from what I have heard he is more than a lunatic—no less than a dangerous madman."

"I will concede that."

"We have no such cases here. My patients are simple souls—mental, true, but absolutely harmless. This is not a lunatic asylum, but a clinic for gentlemen suffering from nerves—slight mental derangement."

"But I noticed the windows are barred?"

"A precaution to prevent wandering. We have several cases of recurring lost memories. In such cases a patient might wander out and get lost. All the bad cases in the county go to Dench. If there is anything in your theory you should visit the County Asylum at Dench."

"Probably I shall do so. But I came here first because it was the nearer."

"I shall be happy to help you all I can, but I fear you will be disappointed."

"Thank you. In the first place, how many patients have you?"

"Sixteen."

"All men—of course?"

"Oh yes."

"They dine together?"

"Usually—in the dining-hall. But if a patient expresses a desire to have his meals in his quarters he does so."

"What kind of quarters are provided?"

"A bedroom, and a private sitting-room. Occasionally more accommodation is given, but very rarely."

"Are there any bicycles in the establishment?"

"Several, I believe, used by members of the staff."

"May I see them?"

"Certainly. There is a special shed in which they are housed. I will send for the porter."

McLean was shown the cycle shed. It contained about half a dozen cycles, but not one of them tallied with the description of the stolen cycle, and four of them belonged to maids employed on the domestic staff of the house. Ultimately McLean returned to the doctor.

"May I ask another favour?"

"As many as you like."

"I should like to see all your patients. I have no desire to question them."

"Certainly. Why not stay to lunch? It is my custom to take that meal with them. You will then have an opportunity of seeing them all together."

McLean accepted. Half an hour later a gong sounded and the patients congregated in the fine dining-room. The doctor introduced McLean as a personal friend, and the patients bowed to him in a cultured way. An excellent meal was served at a long table, and McLean found ample scope for human analysis. The company was extremely well-behaved. They chatted together, and cracked a few jokes. The man next him engaged him in conversation about the opera, and displayed a wide knowledge of the subject.

McLean turned his attention to one patient after another, and finally became interested in a big man sitting at the end of the table. He was quite young—not more than thirty, and possessed a chest like a bull, great muscular arms, and a stubborn jaw. Unlike most of the others he talked little, and seemed to be lost in thought.

" Who is the big man at the end ? " asked McLean of the doctor.

" Gwenn. A comparatively new arrival. Somnambulistic—a little moody, but a charming personality."

" How long has he been here ? "

" Six weeks."

" Ah ! "

After the meal the party adjourned to the lounge for coffee. McLean deliberately sought a seat near the burly Gwenn. Two men opposite commenced a game of chess, and McLean seized that opportunity to try out a subtle test. He possessed a pair of glasses, which he used for close reading. These he took from their case, polished them rather obtrusively under Gwenn's nose, and donned them—apparently to watch the chess-players. But he saw nothing of the game. Although his head was inclined towards the chess-board, his eyes were regarding Gwenn.

The big man became restive. McLean saw his hands close and unclose. McLean took the glasses with his left hand, and rubbed his eyes with his right. The left hand " accidentally " found its way towards Gwenn. There was a rapid movement. The big fingers of the stalwart patient made a dive, but halted in mid-air—almost touching the glasses.

" I beg your pardon ! " said McLean, and donned the glasses again.

A few minutes later he stole away and found the doctor.

" Well, my dear Inspector, are you satisfied ? "

" Quite ! " replied McLean. " I have found the man I want, but I need proof. That I hope to get— very soon."

§

Two days later McLean started a new vocation— warden in the clinic of Dr. du Park. The specialist was ready to lend him every assistance, but it was obvious that he thought McLean was making a great mistake, and he did not know for certain which of his patients was under suspicion.

McLean found his new job full of interest. The patients understood that he had come there at the doctor's behest to study cases, and most of them were fully aware of their trouble, and only too eager to discuss it. But Gwenn never talked about his trouble. As the doctor had stated, he was moody. There were times when he was quite normal and full of high spirits, and times when he sought his room and refused to see anyone. It was to Gwenn that McLean gave all his attention. After the exhibition of wonderful patience he wormed himself into Gwenn's confidence. The man was poor, and the big fees were being paid by his uncle. He was an inventor, he said, but his health had broken down. Was McLean interested in inventions?

"Very. I have always been interested in optics."

Gwenn's eyes lighted up.

"Coincidence! So am I. One day I'll show you something."

McLean knew better than to push the matter further at that moment, but one evening Gwenn came to him again. It was evident he was in the throes of one of his bad attacks, for his eyes were constantly on the move, and his voice husky.

"You've got some glasses?"

"Yes."

"Will you give them to me?"

"But I need them myself."

"I'll pay for them—when I get some money. They're bound to send me some money soon. I wrote again last night. I want the glasses—I must have them."

"What do you want them for?"

He put one huge finger to the side of his nose.

"A secret. But I'll show you—if you give me your glasses."

"All right. Here they are."

Gwenn seized the glasses as if they were jewels of priceless value. He then beckoned McLean towards his sitting-room, and McLean entered it. There was nothing extraordinary about the room itself. It was like all the other rooms in the establishment—large and quite well furnished. Gwenn went to a cupboard and took out a long box in both arms. He laid it on the table and unlocked it with a small key which he kept in his waistcoat pocket. But he did not raise the lid at once.

"You can't guess," he said. "You haven't an idea."

"No, I haven't."

"It's a—boomoscope."

"A what?"

"A boomoscope—the result of years of experiment. It isn't ready yet—not quite. When it is it will startle the world. Through it one will be able to see the future. You see, there is no such thing as Time. Everything is stationary—we just move through events, and we get the idea that it is the events that are moving. Just like being in an express train, and watching the fields and cattle slip by. I'll show you."

He raised the lid, and McLean craned his neck forward. Inside the box, set in a sheet of cardboard with the aid of sealing-wax, were dozens of lenses, obviously taken from spectacles and eye-glasses. There were other things too—some wires and part of a small telescope.

"Fine!" said McLean seriously. "But doesn't it work?"

"Not yet—but it will. I want twenty more lenses and I haven't the money. I shall have to get them—to get them——"

"How?"

"They will come. I know—I know."

McLean gasped when he got outside. Things were getting clearer and clearer. Here was the motive for crime—the motive created by an unbalanced brain. But he wanted to add the last link—to locate the bicycle. He went into the grounds and approached the barred windows of Gwenn's apartments. The window of the sitting-room had not been tampered with, but among the bars of the bedroom window was one which could be removed. The window being divided by a beam, the bars were of short length and painted white. Here, without doubt, was the weapon used!

McLean examined it closer. It surprised him that Gwenn could get his big form through the orifice created by the removal of one bar, but it was certain he did so. In two places there were dark stains—very faint, as if they had been wiped away while the blood was yet wet!

Sergeant Brook was called on the telephone. He arrived at the house dressed in plain clothes, as instructed, and found McLean looking very contented. Brook knew that look. It signified that the job was practically finished.

"I've got him, Brook, but I need to find the bicycle. He will doubtless lead us to it very shortly. I want you to watch the place from outside from seven o'clock till midnight each day. He may succeed in eluding me. If he goes for the cycle, nab him when he handles it. And take care— he is both big and dangerous."

"I'll watch him, sir."

McLean continued to keep a lynx-like watch on Gwenn, but for several evenings he was busy in his room on the "boomoscope." Then the thing happened! Immediately after dinner one night Gwenn went to his room. McLean followed him, and knocked on the door. No answer came, but McLean thought he heard the sound of a window being raised. He ran along the corridor and made into the park. On rounding the house he saw Gwenn on the branch of a tall pine tree, near the spiked wall. He ran along this like a monkey, and when he reached the end of it, jumped clean over the wall. The feat was beyond McLean's capabilities, so he made for the main gate, and got into the road by that means.

But Gwenn had gone into the darkness, and it

was impossible to know which direction he had taken. McLean walked along the road looking everywhere. A quarter of an hour must have passed, and then he saw a figure running towards him. It was Gwenn. He passed McLean two hundred yards to his right and made for the wall surrounding the mansion. A tremendous leap gave him finger-hold between the spikes, and with herculean efforts he was up and over.

"McLean!"

It was Brook's voice. He came out of the gloom wheeling a bicycle—a green bicycle. When he reached McLean, in a breathless state, McLean saw that his head was bleeding.

"Are you hurt?"

"He nearly copped me. I put my hand up in time and partly broke the blow. I didn't bargain for his strength, and I didn't like to shoot. Poor devil!"

"Are you all right?"

"Yes, and this is the bike or I'm a Dutchman. Where did he go?"

"Back into the house. Leave the cycle at the lodge. We'll get him in his rooms."

On reaching the house McLean posted Brook at the main entrance. He decided that the two of them were quite capable of dealing with the lunatic, and desired to avoid any "scene" among the patients.

"I hope to get him quietly," he said. "If not I'll whistle for you. If I miss him and you see him, get him if you can—uninjured. But you must shoot if absolutely necessary."

"Very good, sir."

McLean entered the house, and made his way to Gwenn's apartment. As he entered the long corridor he saw Gwenn at the end of it, about to mount the stairs.

"Mr. Gwenn!"

The lunatic never turned his head, but commenced mounting the stairs at a furious pace. McLean went after him. There were six stories in the building and Gwenn went through all of them. On the sixth McLean called to him again, but he mounted a ladder at the end of the corridor and unbolted a trap-door which led on to the flat roof. McLean hesitated for a moment and then followed him.

A big clear moon had risen, and the scene was a beautiful one, for the whole landscape was flooded with mysterious moonlight. McLean saw Gwenn surveying the coast from the shallow coping— standing quite still as if under a spell. He approached him from the rear.

"Mr. Gwenn!"

Gwenn jumped like a cat, and began to circle round McLean. His eyes were strangely illumined, and he was muttering to himself.

"Come down," begged McLean. "I'd like to have another look at your boomoscope. I've found another pair of spectacles."

"Eh?"

"They're downstairs. I have been looking for you."

"Spectacles—more lenses!" He laughed insanely. "We'll go. So we will. But not down that silly staircase. I've got an idea—we'll jump down—ever so much quicker. We'll jump on the flower-bed—the big round one—down there."

McLean now had his back towards the coping, and Gwenn was pressing him, and pointing down with his finger. It was a hundred feet sheer, and only the short coping intervened!

"Oh no!" said McLean. "That's foolish."

"It would be clever to land right on the flower-bed. Not so easy from this height. You go first and I'll see if I can beat you."

McLean shook his head, and the lunatic glared. He came forward with glowering eyes—an immense figure rigid with determination. McLean's hand went to his pocket, and then he made an alarming discovery. He had forgotten to change over the pistol when he changed his clothes before dinner! Fit and agile as he was, he knew he stood no chance in a physical combat with the lunatic, and there was no way of escape, for he was now hemmed in the corner formed by two sides of the coping.

" Jump ! " snarled Gwenn.

" Not me," retorted McLean calmly. " Any fool could do a trick like that. A small child could do it. Look ! "

He flung down a box of matches, and Gwenn followed its course in the bright moonlight with wondering eyes. It was evident he was now completely crazy—dangerous, yet harmless so long as he was humoured.

" I'll tell you a better trick," mused McLean. " We'll go down by the staircase, and then jump up."

" Jump up ! How ? "

" Oh, it's easy enough when you know how. I'll show you the way. And we'll bring everyone out to see us do it. What do you think of that for an idea ? "

" Yes—yes. Fetch 'em out—bring 'em out ! "

McLean nodded and found his police whistle. He blew it with all his might. Gwenn, in a state of wild excitement, snatched it from him, and blew it again and again—louder than McLean thought was possible. Then, grabbing McLean's arm, he dragged him towards the ladder. They descended at breakneck speed from the roof to the sixth floor, then to the fifth and fourth. On turning from the landing of the fourth they came face to face with Brook.

" Get him, Brook ! "

There was a fearful struggle as Brook leapt at the big lunatic. To threaten him with the pistol was useless. He had to be handcuffed. To do this Brook knocked him out with the neatest of uppercuts, while McLean hung on to the two great arms. The handcuffs were slipped on, and later his legs were manacled.

The next day Gwenn was removed to an asylum for criminal lunatics, and the green bicycle was returned to its rightful owner.

McLEAN INVESTIGATES 11

§

AMONG McLean's treasures was a Crooks' Encyclopædia of his own compiling. It gave the names of a multitude of men and women who were known to have adopted crime as a serious profession. Some of them had already paid large premiums, others had been more fortunate. Those who had paid the ultimate price were marked with a black star. The lucky ones—those fortunate few who had managed to steer clear of both jail and gallows—were indicated by a red cross.

A considerable amount of information was appended—appearance, habits, peculiarities, *modus operandi*, rendezvous, et cetera. Some of these items were supplied by McLean s confrères, others were due entirely to his own investigations. Some were credited with crimes that had never been brought home to them, and in all probability never would. When McLean had moments of leisure on his hands he would ramble through the book and keep his memory green.

The largest red star in the volume was inscribed against the name of Van Duran. According to the appended notes, Van Duran was born in Amsterdam of quite respectable parents. At the age of sixteen he engaged in the pleasant art of forgery in Italy. Later he turned his hand to engraving, with the result that many more notes appeared in Paris and elsewhere than ever were issued by the Bank of France.

For a period of ten years nothing was recorded against Van Duran, and then he cropped up again in London. McLean knew him quite well, as did many other police officers. A cultured, charming personage, he passed in society as a perfectly respectable bachelor of means. Only the police and Van Duran's accomplices knew the truth.

But the trouble was to produce any kind of evidence that would put Van Duran where he deserved to be. He knew quite well that he was suspected and watched, but he never permitted himself to get flustered. It was just a battle of wits, and so far his wits had served him well.

" I ran into Van Duran just now," said Sergeant

Brook, one morning. "Looked as posh as ever. Morning coat, silk hat, white spats—and a lady."

"*Really* a lady?"

"Well, she looked it, but I expect she's one of those women he gets hold of—to pull his chestnuts out of the fire for him."

"Did he recognise you?"

"Didn't he just! Van would pick out a bad quid at a mile distant. He went into the Carlton, and I popped in too. We met in the Gent's Toilet. He asked me to give you his kindest regards."

McLean smiled. That was like Van Duran.

"Clever devil!" he mused. "I wonder what he is up to at the moment?"

"I found out he was living at the Carlton. Does himself darn well for what he is."

"We'll land him one day," said McLean. "He's getting just a little too bold. While he played a strictly solo game he was pretty safe, but now he is getting lazy, and employing women and men. They'll let him down."

Brook seemed to have his doubts. On various occasions they had been near to getting Van Duran, but always there was a bad snag. He was a heroic kind of crook, with refined tastes. Any show of brute force was out of the question with him. He relied entirely upon his brains—his ability to foresee any weaknesses in his schemes, and a marvellous capacity for covering his tracks.

It was some three weeks later that McLean made rather a smart capture. He suspected a certain man of having been implicated in a robbery at a West End jeweller's, and upon searching the man's lodgings he found a quantity of the missing property. In addition he found some memoranda which convinced him that the man was in close touch with Van Duran. Unfortunately he had no specimen of Van Duran's handwriting, but he decided to carry out a bit of bluff with a view to getting closer to the man who had slipped through the net so many times. What puzzled the prisoner was how McLean had come to know that he had a hand in the recent robbery, and McLean decided to play up to this curiosity.

He paid a visit to the prisoner one morning, with the apparent object of making inquiries about another man who was wanted, and found the prisoner sullen and dejected. He knew nothing about the man mentioned by McLean, but was still curious about the method by which the police had got him.

" Someone must have blabbed," he growled. " That was a pretty neat job."

" I give you credit for that. The trouble is, my dear fellow, you keep such doubtful company. They say there is honour among thieves, but I haven't seen much of it myself."

" You ought to preach, when you come here asking me to squeal on others."

"Not on your friends. I thought you might like to put a spoke in the wheels of dangerous competitors. However, we'll let it go. Take my advice and plead guilty."

"Oh, I know what I'm in for. I've had a good run, and can't complain. And I guess I'd be running now if it wasn't for some dirty squealer."

"You might."

"Who was he, anyway? Come on—just out of curiosity?"

McLean hesitated and then produced a sheet of paper from his pocket. On it was written the prisoner's address—nothing more—in handwriting which corresponded exactly with that of the memoranda found in the prisoner's lodgings.

"That's all," said McLean. "Anonymous."

The prisoner's eyes blazed with hate as he stared at the writing.

"Him! By gosh, and I thought he was straight! Well, I can wait. When I come out I'll deal with him."

"So you know him?"

"You bet I do. Well, I won't get more than two years. After that he'd better look out for himself."

McLean said nothing, but he realised the depth of the prisoner's hate for the man whom he believed had given him away to serve some personal end, and he was prepared to wait patiently until the poison had sunk even deeper. That happened when the prisoner was committed to penal servitude for five years. McLean made a point of seeing him before he left.

"They made it hot for you," he said, with a trace of sympathy in his voice. "When you come out, take my advice, and keep away from certain people. You know who?"

"Keep away! Do you think I'm going to lie still after what I've been let in for? Not much. I'll tell you something. It was a man named Van Duran who sent you that note. I've worked for him at times. He's on a big job now—didn't tell me himself, but I got it through a woman he's thick with. He's after the Connington jewels. You know Connington, the big art collector? There's a scheme in the wind. I don't know what it is—but Van Duran doesn't waste his time on useless stunts. He means to get those gems. There's a woman in it named Lydia—poses as a Hungarian Countess, and also a man. If you can get Van Duran first it will save me the job of bashing him. Good-bye; you're not a bad sort —for a cop."

That was the last that McLean saw of the irate cat-burglar. Presuming the information he had received was reliable, it gave him a tremendous advantage. It was the first time in his career that he had received advance notice of one of Van

Duran's exploits, and it put the battle on a level footing. But he did not make the mistake of under-rating the cunning of the man he was after. There would be no bungling in that quarter. Whatever was in the wind would be cleverly planned and executed in masterly style.

Brook and another man took on the job of shadowing Van Duran, while McLean paid a visit to Sir George Connington—famous as the possessor of an incomparable art collection. Among other things he collected precious stones, and had a weakness for rubies. His home was in Berkshire—a magnificent mansion in a beautiful park. McLean found him in his library, looking over some recently acquired treasures.

" Ah, Inspector McLean ! " he said. " I scarcely expected a visit from the police. What have I done now ? "

" Nothing serious, Sir George. It has come to our knowledge that certain persons are rather interested in your jewels, and it might be advisable to take extra precautions against theft."

" Thank you. As a matter of fact this house is as safe as the Bank of England. I dare anyone to step foot inside it, after I have retired, without awakening the whole countryside. I believe that fact is well known in crook circles."

" Possibly. But I can assure you that there is a person deeply interested who may be clever enough to overcome all your burglar-proof devices. Is it true you are giving a party on the tenth of this month ? "

" Yes."

" A large gathering ? "

" Fairly. About a hundred all told."

" People intimately known to you ? "

" Most of them. There will be a few introductions."

" May I suggest that I am present on that evening —in some private capacity ? "

" If you really have cause to believe that this threat to my property is genuine ? "

" I do."

" Then I shall be grateful to have you on the spot. How shall I introduce you ? "

" An American friend—Studeley. I will write it down. James B. Studeley of Boston."

§

Sir George's party was a bright affair. McLean in the part of a Boston aristocrat was immense. His first surprise came very early in the evening, when he saw no other person than Van Duran standing quite near him, talking to a tall, dark woman of alluring beauty.

" Have I introduced you to Mr. Van Duran ? " inquired Sir George. " Charming man. Speaks

c

every language on earth. Mr. Van Duran—my friend James Studeley, from Boston. Oh, and the Countess Lydia Krafting."

The Countess bowed and went off with Sir George. But Van Duran stayed and smiled at McLean.

"For shame, McLean," he said. "You spoil the whole taste of the place. Surely no one in this highly respectable ménage is under suspicion?"

"Oh, no. I am taking a day off. That is all."

"A policeman's holiday, eh?"

"Something like that. Have you seen the collection of gems? I hear they are rather fine."

"So I understand. What do you think of the Countess? Fine-looking woman—what?"

"I really didn't notice. Probably I shall have more opportunity at a later date."

Van Duran laughed, for he could appreciate a joke of that sort. A little later he joined the Countess, and led her away into a secluded spot.

"Do you know who that was I spoke to just now?" he rapped.

"That—Mister Studeley?"

"Studeley be damned! That was McLean of Scotland Yard. The smartest man in the force. Now, who the devil put him wise to this affair?"

"You think he suspects?"

"Of course he does. He's been after me for years."

" Will he warn Sir George—about us ? "

" No. That wouldn't serve any purpose. What he is after is a capture—in other words *me*, and I intend he shall not have that pleasure."

" You mean you will drop the scheme ? "

" Drop it ! I'm going to pull it off—in my own way. And rather a neat way too. You just carry on as if nothing were amiss. Don't let McLean rattle you."

The self-styled Countess nodded, but she looked a little less sure of herself. Later McLean danced with her, and she had an opportunity to survey him at close range. Her knowledge of men told her Van Duran was up against a big intelligence, and yet her faith in the arch-thief was still great. Even she did not know by what means he intended to possess himself of the priceless collection of gems. She merely had certain work to do—certain information to extract from her host.

All the guests saw the jewel collection later in the evening. McLean watched Van Duran and the Countess, and saw their irrepressible covetousness. Afterwards the collection was housed in a big safe, which was provided with marvellous locks. Sir George was proud of his strong-room, and pointed out to McLean its various locks and devices.

" Rather thief-proof, eh ? "

McLean smiled and shook his head.

" I will undertake to produce at least three men

in London alone who would laugh at all your locks. Is it true you are going abroad shortly?"

"Yes."

"Then don't rely on your strong-room. There is a better one at Rawlings'—the safe deposit people. Even that is not absolutely burglar proof. They know it and employ two very capable night-watchmen. This is an era of Science, and the modern burglar takes advantage of the very latest inventions."

Sir George was rather impressed by this, and before the party broke up he told McLean that he had decided to take his advice when he left England. Nothing happened that night, save that the Countess got on most excellent terms with her host—which was exactly what McLean expected would happen.

"Wonderful woman!" said Sir George. "So full of life—and so charming."

"Have you known her long?"

"Oh, no. A month or so. I forget how we met. She comes of an old Hungarian family. Quite wealthy I believe."

McLean marvelled at Sir George's lack of perception, but made no attempt to disillusion him. Instead he had the place well watched, and also the movements of Van Duran and the Countess.

"Connington took that woman to dine this

evening," said Brook, a few days later. "She went back to the Carlton afterwards."

"Van Duran is still there?"

"Yes."

"Don't lose sight of him."

Three days later the famous jewel collection of Sir George was boxed and lodged with Rawlings' Safe Deposit. It bore many bands and locks, all of which carried Sir George's seal. The owner came to McLean later.

"I feel more relieved now," he said. "And I want to thank you for your suggestion. I suppose it would have been risky to have left them in the house. Servants are careless these days."

"How long shall you be away?"

"Three to four months."

"So there has been no attempt at robbery at your home?"

"None. The intending thief has lost his last opportunity—for three months at least."

McLean was inclined to take that view, but he still kept Van Duran under observation, and also his beautiful female companion. It was now known that the Countess was living in a quite large house near Sloane Square, and that Van Duran visited her at times. Van Duran himself still stayed at the Carlton, and continued to pose as a man about town.

"Nothing doing," mused Brook. "He just

lounges. Theatres, clubs, restaurants. I guess he has retired from business."

"Men like Van Duran never retire—until retirement is enforced by other people."

"Well, we busted his big game anyway. He hadn't the nerve to try his hand on the Connington stuff after he spotted you."

McLean reserved further comment, but he did not relax his efforts to get Van Duran for some offence. The fact that Van Duran was still hand in glove with the Countess led him to believe that some scheme was in the wind. Van Duran had small use for women in his leisure moments.

One day Brook came in with the news that Van Duran had left the Carlton. Inquiries as to his whereabouts had been made, but he had left no address to which any letters might be forwarded. Like a ghost he had vanished into thin air.

"That's a nuisance," said McLean. "I told you to watch him. There were two of you."

"I did all that a human being could do," grumbled Brook. "I fixed things with the day and night porters, and also several others. It appears he left late at night, without giving a minute's notice. Just paid his bill and sloped off by a back exit. He must have known he was being watched."

"Where is Summers now?"

" Watching the Countess' house—in the hope of seeing him there."

" That's all right. Get on to his clubs, Brook, and also the places he habitually visits. There's something maturing."

But although Brook spent all the rest of the day making furtive inquiries, no news of any kind came in regard to the sinister Van Duran. That evening McLean did a bold thing. First of all he secured a warrant to search the house of the Countess, but he did not make use of it in the orthodox manner. Shortly after eleven o'clock he visited the house and entered it by a basement window.

The servants had retired, but there was a light on the ground floor, and another in the hall. He made his way to the ground floor, and saw a hat-stand near the front door. On a peg was a silk hat of the latest pattern. He picked it up and looked inside it. On the lining was inscribed V. D. Listening at various doors he at last came to one from behind which came the sound of low voices. To catch any words was most difficult, but he did manage to overhear a few broken sentences.

" Gaspard will fetch it. . . . Only a day—you must come back unexpectedly."

" Shall I see you here ? " asked the Countess.

" Of course. I ought to have a bottle of something. . . . There'll be no hitch. . . . When all is clear, rap ' O.K.' in Morse. I shall hear."

"It will be heavy."

"Naturally. Silver always is."

"Silver! I like that! Ma chère—you are clever!"

They laughed together, and the "clink" of glasses followed. McLean concluded they must have changed their positions in the room, for the ensuing conversation was not quite audible. Ten minutes later he left the house.

Silver! What did silver mean? And the business about a bottle? Also there was Gaspard, who was going to fetch something—something that was very heavy? Obviously Gaspard was the unknown man mentioned by the recently convicted friend of Van Duran—possibly posing as servant in the house of the Countess! Things were warming up. By eight o'clock the next morning McLean had hit upon a possible solution.

§

At eight o'clock came the first corroboration of his theory. A message arrived from Brook to the effect that the Countess had left her house in a hired car and had gone to Charing Cross Station. Brook was now on the station awaiting developments. Later he telephoned to say that the Countess was travelling to Paris. McLean pursed his lips, and told Brook to come to the office as soon as the

Countess had left in the boat-train. Brook arrived in due course.

"She went," he said.

"Of course she did—as far as Dover."

"Eh?"

"Oh, never mind. Naturally you left the house unwatched in your zest to see what the dear Countess was up to?"

"Well, you told me——"

"Quite right! It doesn't matter very much. We have other means of establishing certain facts. Our friend Van Duran is an ingenious devil, but this time his goose is cooked."

"You—you know where he is?"

"I have a very shrewd idea, but when dealing with a man of that calibre it is never wise to be too sanguine. I fancy I shall need you to-morrow morning, Brook. No, you needn't watch the house any more."

Brook went away extremely puzzled, and McLean took the next step to prove his theory. He went to Rawlings' Safe Deposit, and interviewed the manager.

"You have a client who calls herself the Countess Lydia Krafting?"

"That is so."

"She has deposited her silver here?"

"Yes."

"For what period?"

"Only for a week or so. She was called to Paris suddenly, and made use of us to safeguard her very valuable antiques."

"I am anxious to see those antiques."

"That is impossible."

"I fancy it is rather a fine collection?"

"I have no means of knowing. My business begins and finishes with safeguarding them."

"Quite. May I rely upon you to notify me when the Countess returns—that is to say, when she gives you notice that she is going to collect her valuables?"

"Certainly."

"That is strictly confidential."

"You may trust me."

On the following day at eleven o'clock McLean was rung up by the manager of the Safe Deposit to be informed that the Countess had been taken ill *en route* for Paris and had had to return to her home. She was sending her servant with the car, and her authority to collect the trunk, within an hour.

"This is where we stand or fall," said McLean to Brook. "I want you, Summers and Daniels, to go to the house. You will not enter it until the car arrives and the trunk is taken off. As soon as that is done, force an entry. I shall be there immediately after."

"Very good, Inspector!"

Brook went off and McLean hired a taxi and drove to a spot from which he could see the Safe Deposit. He kept the taxi waiting there. After a lapse of twenty minutes a big car drew up at the Safe Deposit. It contained two men—the chauffeur and a swarthy man, presumably Gaspard. There was a delay of a few minutes, and then Gaspard appeared, directing two porters who were handling a very large trunk bearing the initials L. K.

The trunk was placed in the back of the car, and immediately it made away. McLean instructed his driver to follow it, and ultimately he saw it stop outside the Countess' house. Near by was a closed car containing Brook and his fellow-officers. McLean left the taxi and joined his men.

"They're taking the trunk inside," said Brook, who was gazing through the rear window of the saloon car.

"Good! Come on—all of you!"

They left the car and walked up the street until they reached the house. The front door was slightly ajar, for the chauffeur who had helped Gaspard to carry the trunk had not yet come out. The four men entered. When they reached the sitting-room, the trunk was deposited in the centre of it, and the Countess was about to dismiss the chauffeur. She did not look a bit ill, and was completely dressed as if on the point of making a journey. The beautiful face went pallid when

McLean stepped forward, and his three subordinates barred the door.

"Good-morning, Countess!" said McLean. "I heard you were indisposed."

"How—how dare you break into my house!" she expostulated.

"I came to assure myself that your silver is quite safe."

He spoke in a very low voice, to suit his own requirements. When she was about to raise her voice again, he silenced her with a wave of his hand, and advanced towards the big trunk. The chauffeur appeared to be astonished at the proceedings, but Gaspard was evidently in the swindle, for he was violently agitated. McLean remembered the broken conversation he had overheard on his previous visit, and the phrase "rap O.K. in Morse. I shall hear." Producing his pistol he rapped the letters on the end of the trunk. A little cry came from the Countess, but he swung round on her and silenced her with the pistol.

There was a slight noise from the inside of the trunk, then a sharp click. The longer side of the trunk sprang outwards, and from its interior emerged—Van Duran. He was on all-fours when he saw McLean.

"Better stand up," said McLean. "That is a most undignified position."

Van Duran rose to his feet. His limbs were

obviously cramped and his expression was one that clearly expressed his bitter disillusionment.

"Brook!"

The sergeant came forward and snapped a pair of handcuffs on Van Duran's wrists. McLean walked up to his glaring prisoner and slipped his hands into his pockets. They were full of precious jewels from diamonds to rubies. In an inside pocket were sealing-wax and a bunch of skeleton keys, also matches. McLean made a neat parcel of the whole lot. He then examined the trunk, but found nothing in it save an empty bottle, which had contained nourishment for Van Duran for some twenty-four hours.

"Rather neat, Van Duran," he said. "You certainly succeeded in getting the Connington jewels, but your ownership was of brief duration. For that temporary pleasure you have paid heavily. Twenty-four hours in that box would have killed most men—even though it possesses ventilation-holes, skilfully concealed. We shall have to send you away for a little holiday, for the good of your health. I am sorry the Countess—I think you said Countess?—I am sorry she will not accompany you. We have another resort specially planned for ladies—of title."

Van Duran frowned and then recovered his equanimity. To him life was a great adventure, and he was inclined to take his defeat philosophically,

"You win this round," he said. "But I doubt not we shall cross swords again, and then——"

"Well, one never knows. Summers, bring those two other men. Countess, you will find a comfortable car waiting outside. And now, Mr. Van Duran, we are all ready."

A short distance away the manager of Rawlings' famous Safe Deposit was writing calmly, oblivious to the fact that the jewel-box of Sir George Connington contained exactly nothing. But the seals might have told their own story, for they now bore no crest!

III

§

THE Felstead murder was one of those cases in which McLean found himself up against a set of apparently contradictory facts, and in which patience and attention to details played the most important parts. Felstead was a quiet little village in the heart of Surrey, and its recent growth was due to a large estate coming into the market and being put up for auction in small lots. On the outskirts of the village a small colony of neat houses and bungalows had slowly accumulated, and the small holdings, ranging from two to twenty acres, were given over chiefly to poultry-farming and quick crops.

It was early in June when Felstead was shocked by a brutal murder. The body of a middle-aged man, named John Daymer, was found in the sitting-room of his small bungalow by the boy who brought the milk from the adjacent farm. Death was due to several deep head wounds apparently inflicted by a heavy, blunt instrument, and upon subsequent investigation the county police had to admit that they were without a clue of any kind as to the identity of the murderer. Scotland Yard was called in, and on the following day Inspector McLean and Sergeant Brook arrived by car at Felstead police station. Brook introduced his chief, and the sergeant in charge shook hands gravely.

"A baffling case, sir. I understand you have read the statements?"

"Yes. I haven't had time to—digest them. I came straight from Guildford to see the body before interment. After that I should like to visit the scene of the crime."

McLean took but a few minutes to view the body. The cause of death was abundantly clear. Daymer had evidently been attacked with dreadful violence, for the right side of his head was battered in, and the doctor had stated that death was instantaneous. The deceased was a well-built fellow of about fifty years of age, with a short beard and bristly moustache—the type of man one would imagine could take care of himself in any scuffle. Obviously he had been taken unawares.

"That's plain enough," mused McLean. "Now the bungalow. Is it far away?"

"A mile and a half."

"We will take the car."

Brook drove carefully down several very narrow, winding lanes and ultimately pulled up, on the instructions of their pilot, at a path which led across a short meadow, beyond which was a new bungalow—standing in a field by itself. The nearest habitation was at least half a mile away, and nearer the village.

"Is this the only entrance?" asked McLean.

"No. There is another further on, but the proposed new road is in a shocking state. Most people use this path."

The local sergeant possessed the key to the door, and they entered the bungalow. It contained a fairly large sitting-cum-dining-room, two small bedrooms, a bathroom and a kitchen. The tragedy had taken place in the sitting-room, and their guide announced that nothing had been disturbed since the time of the discovery. All the police had done was to take the body away.

McLean nodded while his eyes took in every detail. In the grate were the remains of a fire, some orange-peel, and an old tobacco-tin. The fender was askew, and on the worn hearth-rug and neighbouring carpet were deep stains.

"We found him lying there," indicated the sergeant. "On his right side, with his head close to the right end of the fender—where the stains are deepest."

"These two chairs were like this—exactly?"

"Yes."

McLean turned to the table. The cloth was pulled half off, and an empty cup, with some dregs of coffee in the bottom, was dangerously near the edge.

"The window was open?"

"Yes. I had to close that afterwards—owing to rain."

"And the door?"

"Closed but unbolted."

"No sign of a forced entry?"

"None."

"I notice you give the motive as robbery?"

"Yes. But there is a doubt. You will see that the bank cashier deposes that deceased cashed a cheque for fifty pounds on the afternoon preceding the crime. But we also have a statement from a young man employed at the Felstead Hotel, who swears that he saw the deceased paying a large sum of money to a stranger in the yard of the hotel late that afternoon."

"What money was found on the body?"

"Six shillings and eightpence."

"Hm! Pretty conclusive!"

The local officer apparently did not agree, but he dared not say so. McLean dismissed him a few minutes later, telling him he would call in on his way back—after he had made further investigations.

"You think it was robbery, sir?" asked Brook.

"I can't imagine a man paying away fifty pounds in cash and leaving himself with six shillings and eightpence. If he had to go to the bank to draw that money—with the intention of paying it all away—it is rather reasonable to expect he would draw a pound or two for himself. I may be wrong. It's just an argument. Don't touch that glass!"

Commenced a hunt for finger-prints, but the closest scrutiny failed to reveal any such thing. The window was a casement, leading into a small flower-garden, and anyone could have entered it by the paved path without leaving a footprint.

"Clues are at a premium, Brook," said McLean. "I have a feeling that the fellow we want is rather a clever scoundrel, and yet he has done a thing that puzzles me."

Brook had scarcely had time to get his breath, leave alone arrive at such a lightning conclusion. He gazed at McLean blankly.

"You don't follow me, Brook?"

"Sorry, sir."

"I am wondering why he should want to dispose of the instrument he used on his victim."

"But isn't that natural?"

"No—not in the circumstances. If it were a personal instrument, yes—but a piece of the furniture——"

"But we don't know——!"

"I think there isn't much doubt. I have been searching for the poker which matches this set of fireirons. It happens to be a practically new set. Shovel, tongs, brush and rack—but no poker. That isn't usual, is it?"

"By Jove—I never thought of that!"

"We'll take concerted action."

They searched every inch of the place but found no sign of the poker.

"Even if he did use the poker, he might take it with him, and discard it later?" suggested Brook.

"It would have been more natural to let it stay. He could have wiped it on the coat of his victim—— Well, we need a fairly stout steel poker as our first exhibit. There's a nice job for you, Brook, while I run into the village. I'll be back in an hour. I rather imagine the murderer left by the window, and there are numerous bushes that would make quite a nice receptacle for such an implement. See you later."

In the village McLean carried out one or two necessary tasks. He ascertained that the money drawn from the bank by the dead man was made up of thirty one-pound notes and four five-pound notes. The numbers of the latter were noted. The boy at the hotel who had seen Daymer in conversation with a stranger was rather a dull-witted fellow. He had the greatest difficulty in describing the man. The only thing he was certain about was that he was middle-aged and wore a light-coloured suit. He saw money passing—and thought it was a big batch, but wasn't sure. It might have been twenty pounds, ten, or even five.

McLean turned his attention to other persons who knew the deceased, but their knowledge of him was scanty. He appeared to be a man who kept his affairs to himself. No one knew where he came from, and he seemed to have no correspondence of any kind. But one thing of importance did emerge. Two men stated that they had seen the deceased wearing a very fine gold-hunter watch on many occasions. This fact the police had not previously discovered. The watch was not included in the things left by the dead man. It established the motive.

McLean went back to the bungalow, and found Brook still searching for the poker.

They spent another hour about the place, and before he left McLean made a small discovery. Attached to a blackberry thorn, near the path that led from the window, was a very small fragment of grey thread. It was little more than an inch long. He took it and placed it in his note-book.

§

Weeks passed and no further progress was made. The poker was searched for diligently but unsuccessfully. The description of the watch and the numbers of the notes were published, but never a sign came throughout the whole summer. Then, in October, one of the missing notes was traced. It was paid to a hotel in York, who banked it on the following day. The bank communicated with Scotland Yard, and McLean went up-country. The hotel cashier was able to identify the man who paid him the note. He was a well-known local bookmaker—and a man of some integrity. He could give no information concerning the note, beyond the fact that it was given him on the race-course on the day he paid it to the hotel in settlement of his bill.

There was nothing against him, and the incident passed. It did not even establish the fact that the murderer was at York races, for the life of a five-pound note was fairly long, and that particular specimen might have passed through a dozen innocent hands before it reached the bookmaker. McLean was thus obliged to sit tight.

Two weeks passed and then a second note was

traced. In this case it came from a tradesman in Sunderland, and it was paid to him by a man named Risler, not long resident in the city. On McLean's instructions Risler was not interrogated at once, but a watch was set on his movements. It was very soon ascertained that Risler had no real occupation. He attended race-meetings, did a little bookmaking and engaged in one or two other speculative enterprises. Further investigations elicited the fact that Risler had served a long stretch of imprisonment fifteen years back for embezzlement, with a man named Grogan.

At this juncture McLean himself took up the threads. For days he watched Risler, and on one occasion he saw him dressed in a suit that corresponded with the description given him by the boy at the Felstead Hotel, and also with the small piece of thread retrieved from the blackberry bush. Risler was followed to his lodgings and there McLean called on him.

" I am a police officer," he said.

Risler raised his eyebrows in apparent astonishment.

" Your name is Mark Risler ? "

" Yes."

" On November the second you paid a five-pound note to a tradesman in Sunderland. Do you recall that ? "

" Yes. I think I do. It was for some whisky."

"How did you come possessed of that note?"

"I must have got it from the bank."

"That was impossible."

"Why?"

"For certain good reasons."

"But I—— Oh, no, I remember now. It was given to me by a man named Grogan—an old pal of mine."

"The man you went to jail with?"

Risler shrugged his shoulders and grinned.

"Well, I admit it. But that is over and done with, and you have no right to bring that up now."

"Why did Grogan give you that note?"

"I met him on his way to France. I had just returned from a flutter at Monte Carlo, where I made a bit of money. He was going to cash some notes for francs and I happened to have a pocket full of them. I did a deal with him, and took his money."

This explanation came quickly and coolly. McLean realised he was dealing with a man of considerable intelligence. He watched him as a cat does a mouse, but detected no sign of nervousness.

"I have a search warrant," he said. "I should like to run over this flat."

"Certainly. Go right ahead! Can I offer you a cigarette?"

"No, thanks."

McLean began his search, and finally, in the back of a deep drawer, he found a gold hunter watch, which corresponded in every detail to the one missing.

" Is this yours ? " he asked.

" Yes."

" How long have you possessed it ? "

" About a month. I did a deal with Grogan at the same time as I changed that note for him. He offered to let me have the watch for six thousand francs, and I knocked him down to five thousand. I don't wear it—too clumsy. I shall sell it when I get a fair offer."

McLean nodded his head and pocketed the watch.

" I am going to arrest you, Mr. Risler," he said.

" Arrest—— ! "

" On the charge of murdering John Daymer in Surrey on the night of June 4."

" You must be mad."

McLean went to the door and gave a whistle. Brook, who had been waiting below, came up the stairs in bounds.

" Handcuffs ! "

Risler looked desperate for a moment, but he recovered his earlier calm and held out his hands.

" You are doing a stupid thing, Inspector," he said. " And you will have cause to regret it."

At headquarters the consensus of opinion was that McLean had acted a little impetuously, for the possession of the watch and the five-pound note seemed thin enough evidence on which to base a very serious charge. There was, too, the short length of grey thread, but expert opinion was not prepared to swear that it came from the grey suit found in Risler's possession. Like a wise man Risler preferred to make no statement.

McLean's next step was an identification test, and while this was being arranged Brook and half a dozen other officers were carrying out a minute search for the missing poker. To McLean's bitter disappointment the identification test gave a negative result. The dull-witted boy from the hotel picked out the wrong man. McLean's heart fell. He had collected a mass of detail about the prisoner, which convinced him of the fellow's guilt, but he saw that unless something more incriminating came to light the charge would fail.

"I want that poker, Brook," he said. "It represents the last scrap of hope. Get more men on the job. We have it on the evidence of a charwoman that the poker was in that room two days before the crime took place."

"It's like looking for a needle in a haystack," grumbled Brook. "If we do find it, it may not help."

McLean realised this. That day a troop of Boy

Scouts were turned out on the quest, and during the evening the telephone bell rang to inform McLean that the article had been found in a thick clump of rhododendrons not a hundred yards from the bungalow.

" Any markings ? "

" Discolorations," said Brook. " Finger-prints too, I believe. I'm bringing it right along."

" Handle it gently for heaven's sake."

An hour later the implement was at Scotland Yard. It was short and rather stout, with the unmistakable stains of blood upon it. So furiously had it been used that it was bent considerably. McLean got to work with a large magnifying-glass, and his eyes lighted up.

" You're right, Brook. Two good impressions here. Now we shall know where we stand ! "

§

The subsequent photographic print showed the impressions clearly, but when McLean came to compare them with the finger-prints of Risler there was no resemblance whatever.

" Confound ! " he muttered.

" Nothing like ! " ejaculated Brook.

" No. Now what the devil—— ? "

" Is he telling the truth ? "

" About his friend—Grogan ? "

"Yes."

"No. There were flaws in that story. Risler has never been to Monte Carlo so far as we can trace. In which case the story of the francs was a lie, and the whole business an invention. Records, Brook. Look up Grogan's record. Let us see where he comes in."

Brook was soon immersed in his job, and at last found details concerning Grogan. There was a photograph, and a fine set of finger-prints, dating back some fifteen years. It was here that McLean suffered a surprise. The finger-prints on the poker were Grogan's without a doubt.

"Gosh! Then Risler didn't lie!" ejaculated Brook.

It was a set-back to McLean. Here was Risler's story absolutely corroborated, and there was nothing so far as McLean could see that would implicate Risler at this juncture. It could not be proved that he knew by what means Grogan gained possession of the watch or the note.

Commenced a search for Grogan, and in the hope of getting some further information about that elusive individual McLean again visited the bungalow, which was still awaiting a claimant. But nothing transpired, and ultimately the police had to face the humiliating prospect of withdrawing the charge. When Risler was informed of this he smiled derisively.

"I have grounds for action," he said. "And I intend to take it."

"That is up to you," replied McLean. "But I should go warily, my friend."

"The police are too cheeky these days. I told you the truth, but you refused to believe me."

"Remember you are known to have received stolen property. When we find Grogan it may still be a little awkward for you."

"Find him first."

"Would it surprise you to learn that he is found?"

Risler started and then shook his head.

"You can't bluff me like that."

"I wouldn't try to bluff a man so clever. It will be interesting to hear Grogan's version of that deal you did with him."

Risler laughed, and McLean felt that his mirth was genuine. It looked as if Risler knew that Grogan could never be found. That point stuck in McLean's mind. When Risler finally walked out of prison, a free man, McLean had him watched, still certain in his mind that Risler had a hand in the murder.

The threatened action against the police did not take place. That was a little significant in the circumstances, for some action would have been expected with a man of Risler's spiteful disposition. No, Mr. Risler was content to let the matter drop.

But McLean was keener than ever to solve this perplexing mystery. He applied to the Passport Office, but their records did not help him trace the wanted man.

McLean turned the matter over and over in his mind. Why was Risler so cocksure that Grogan would never be found? Was it due to the fact that Grogan was no longer in the land of the living? A startling idea then came to him. It was gruesome but not impossible. Risler might have done the murder and used a severed hand to make the imprints on the poker before it was discarded—knowing that in the long run it must be found. To have left it on the scene of the murder would have been too obvious. It was fantastic. Would any man come armed with such a gruesome thing, ready to scatter a red-herring across the trail? No, that did not fit. The story as he saw it was a little different. The murderer had come to collect some money from the deceased. This had been paid to him, but his greed had been aroused by the sight of a wallet full of notes. He had waited about until after dark, and then called on his intended victim—a call that had the appearance of being quite friendly. The unsuspecting victim had given his visitor a chair by the fire. Suddenly the murderer had snatched up the poker and committed his dastardly crime. And then——

McLean's eyes lighted up. In a second he saw

it all. It accounted for everything—including certain resemblances. He looked up documents, photographs—and at last he knew he was right. That evening he had an interview with his " chief."

" I want an exhumation order, sir."

" In what matter ? "

" John Daymer."

" But on what grounds ? "

" I believe John Daymer to be none other than John Grogan."

" Grogan ! The man whom we want for the—— Great heavens, that is an extraordinary theory."

" It is more than a theory. Look at these photographs. One taken fifteen years ago, the other recently. Allow for the passage of years—the growth of the beard and moustache. The physical details are identical."

" But the poker bore the finger-prints of Grogan ! "

" Yes. That is the vital point, sir."

The " chief " gasped. It was a totally unexpected shot. An application was made to the right quarter, and forty-eight hours later McLean and Sergeant Brook were rushing up-country.

" We're going to get Risler again ? " asked Brook.

" We are, and this time for keeps."

" But—— ! "

McLean lighted a cigarette and pointed out an

interesting bit of geology to his bewildered assistant.

"Ought to be a lot of Palæolithic records in that district," he mused. "Must pay it a visit when I get a holiday."

"Palæolithic be blow———? Did Risler do that job after all?"

"He did. I rather admire his cunning. Ought to have been put to better use."

They found Risler that night, sitting in his flat, drinking and reading the evening newspaper. He gazed at them in amazement as they entered unannounced.

"Mr. Risler, I have a second warrant for your arrest," said McLean.

"I—I won't submit to this. It is outrageous!"

"I am afraid you will have to. I must warn you that anything you may say——"

"Oh, to blazes with your warnings. Is this a new charge?"

"It is. The exact charge is—the murder of Mr. John Grogan at——"

A look of terror passed over Risler's face. Suddenly he dived for the drawer of a bureau, but Brook got there first, and two seconds later he was handcuffed. That night he was lodged in a cell, and McLean went home feeling that at last justice was going to triumph.

But Risler's brain served him to the end. On

the following morning he was found in his bed—dead. He had broken the electric-light globe, and with a sharp fragment of glass had opened an artery in his left wrist. A book was lying beside him, and in the margin was inscribed in his own blood his confession.

"I killed John Grogan. I had an old score to pay, and after missing him for many years I ran him to earth that day at Felstead. He gave me twenty pounds to get out of the country, but I saw he had a wallet full of money. I waited for some hours and then called on him, pretending I had missed my train. I hit him several times with the poker. He put his hands to his head and they became covered with blood. It was then I thought of the idea of pressing his hands on the end of the poker—before I hid it where I knew it would be found later. In the event of my being traced I had a good story, and I knew that Scotland Yard had Grogan's finger-prints. It was the smartest thing I ever did—and yet it failed. My compliments to McLean. But I'm beating him now.

"MARK RISLER."

"I admit defeat when it saves the country so much money," commented McLean. "The trial might have lasted a long time. But in the end I daresay a sensible jury would have found him guilty. The trouble with him was—he was just a little too ingenious. A deplorable end to a life that might have been useful."

Three hours later McLean was in the neighbourhood of Hampstead on the track of a very rare and elusive beetle. He really preferred that to manhunting, for the odds were always on the beetle.

McLEAN INVESTIGATES — IV

§

IT wasn't often that Sergeant Brook found real trouble. His long experience in the Force and his herculean physique combined to make him a formidable adversary. But like many other guardians of the law he had made a few enemies, and among these was " Stiff " Colyer.

Colyer was an accomplished crook and an impenitent scoundrel. He had served many minor sentences until seven years before when he was arrested by Brook and charged with serious assault and battery. For seven long and weary years " Stiff " had languished in Princetown Jail, which to a man of his prodigious activity was positive hell. McLean on reading some official documents one morning came upon the name of " Stiff " Colyer.

"An old friend of yours, Brook," he remarked.

"Who?"

"Colyer. He left prison yesterday."

"I'll bet he'll soon be back again."

"I've no doubt, but I should be wary of him if I were you. He's a vindictive brute and is capable of any kind of villainy."

"He certainly doesn't love me," laughed Brook. "But if he starts any rough stuff it will be his funeral."

McLean glanced at Brook's huge frame. The sergeant was reputed to be the toughest man in the division. He was a splendid boxer, a fine wrestler, and an all-round athlete. But now he was past his prime—though still as fit as a fiddle.

"All the same, it isn't wise to disregard Colyer's threats. He's a crack shot and would smell you at a distance."

But Brook, possessing less knowledge of human psychology, did not take "Stiff's" open threats seriously. A man who could beat an old woman into unconsciousness and rob her of a few pounds was not the sort of creature to arouse any fears in his breast. He therefore went about his business and forgot the matter.

A month passed, during which time both Brook and McLean were hot on the trail of a gang of counterfeiters, only to be led constantly into blind alleys. Brook, in plain clothes, was returning home after participating in an abortive raid at a night club, when a taxi passed him and a woman emerged from it about fifty yards ahead of him. She seemed very unsteady as she paid the driver, and Brook concluded she had been having a gay time. The taxi made off as he approached her, and as she moved towards the entrance to the big block of flats she staggered and fell heavily.

Brook hurried forward and leaned over her. But he could not detect any odour of drink, and now realised that she was ill. After a few seconds she opened her eyes and stared up into his face. He saw that she was young and very pretty—also well dressed.

" Where——? What——? " she gasped.

" You fainted," he said. " Are you feeling better ? "

" I—I think so. Everything seemed to spin round. My—my heart has been troubling me. Thank you ! "

With the aid of his arm she stood up, but continued to cling to him as if she feared to walk alone. She passed her hand across her forehead.

" I—live here. I—think I can manage."

But it was evident she could not, for immediately she let go of his arm she tottered alarmingly, and had to grab the iron railings by the side of the few steps in order to steady herself.

" Where is your apartment ? " asked Brook.

"First floor."

"Isn't there a lift?"

"No. But I shall be all right in a minute. I had an attack—like this—last week."

She managed to mount the steps, but at the top she was breathing with great difficulty, and fumbling in her bag for the latch-key.

"Let me help you," said Brook.

He had almost to lift her up the long flight of stairs, and at the top she indicated her door. Again she fumbled for the key, and then suddenly collapsed again, her handbag falling by the side of her. It was open and the key was visible. Brook took it and opened the door. Inside was a large bed-sitting room. He turned to the recumbent girl and lifted her inside and on to the bed. Her slim hands were tearing at the neck of her silk jumper. There was a ripping of silk and a white neck came to view. She now seemed to breathe easier.

"Better?" asked Brook.

"A—little. I—I think I should like to see my doctor. There's a telephone. Please—please ring. Doctor Rushton—the number is on the card."

Brook found the number and tried to call the exchange, but could get no response. Again and again he tried. Ultimately he turned his head and saw the girl's hair all dishevelled and the bed untidy.

"Why, what——?" he commenced.

The door suddenly opened and an exceedingly big man entered the room. He was ten years younger than Brook, with an immense head and iron jaw. He looked at the girl and then at Brook.

" Carl ! "

The man's face tightened and he closed the door firmly and turned the key in the lock.

" So I've caught you this time ? "

Brook frowned and looked towards the girl, expecting her to explain matters. But she made not the slightest attempt to do so. Instead she stood up and looked at the new-comer defiantly.

" What's all this ? " said Brook. " Are you this lady's husband ? "

" I am," snarled Carl. " And you are going to know it."

" Wait ! She was taken ill and I——"

" Ill ! Does she look ill ? Don't try to pull any of that stuff over me. I've suspected this for some time, and now I'm going to give you a lesson."

He flung off his coat and rolled up his shirt-sleeves. Brook saw a pair of magnificent arms, and knew what he was up against. The nose, the jaw, the whole muscular lay-out of the man showed at once that he was a trained pugilist—a most formidable heavy-weight. On the left forearm was a tattooed anchor.

" Carl ! " said the girl.

"Shut your jaw! You can pick up the pieces when I've finished."

He advanced on Brook, poised lightly on his toes—the embodiment of human grace. Brook was quick at sizing up such men. He knew he had no earthly chance against this fellow. He might as well have matched himself against Dempsey or Tunney. Here was a man in the very prime—a regular fighting machine. But Brook was not the type of man to howl for quarter. He saw the "plant" now, and was prepared to pay the price of his indiscretion. McLean had warned him, and yet he had stepped into the trap like a brainless fly.

"Put 'em up—you skunk!"

Brook had only just time to do so, in order to avoid a lightning hook to the jaw. His blood was fired now, and he fought with all the skill and desperation at his command. But it was almost a battle of complete defence. He was utterly outclassed, and being rapidly exhausted by the enormous pace of his opponent. Once only did he manage to get in a hard body punch, and this seemed to shake Carl for a few seconds, but soon the ferocious attack began to break through. Brook took punches everywhere. Blood began to flow. His face swelled up—and yet he fought on doggedly.

All the time the girl watched the extraordinary scene, combing her hair at intervals. Brook felt he would have liked to land one of his blows on a certain part of her anatomy, but his time was too occupied. Thwack! A heavy blow landed on his jaw. He reeled away but managed to avoid a knock-out. Now he fell, now he was up again. Valiant fighter as he was, the end was inevitable. Any referee would have stopped such a fight, but Brook still fought on until at last he was gasping for breath. He saw Carl manœuvring for the knock-out, and at last it came. With a terrible crash the sergeant measured his length on the floor and lay quite still.

On the following morning McLean arrived at the office to find Brook absent. He was about to make some inquiries when Inspector Day entered the room.

"Have you heard about Brook?" he asked.

"No. I was just about to inquire."

"He was found by a constable at one o'clock this morning with his face bashed in. The constable found him in a half-conscious condition propped up against the railings near Frith Street. He took him home. He lives quite near."

"Great Scott! That's bad. Has Brook made any statement?"

"Not yet."

"I'll run along and see him."

McLean found his subordinate in an unsightly condition. There were strips of sticking-plaster all over his big face, and one eye was badly cut and swollen. He greeted McLean with an embarrassed smile and continued bathing the injured eye.

"What happened?" asked McLean.

"I stepped into the net—like a darned child."

"Stiff Colyer got you?"

"Not 'Stiff' himself. He couldn't have done this to me. I'm thinking it was a pal of his."

"Tell me what happened."

Brook dried his tender eye and related briefly his experience of the night before.

"And the rotten part is I can't do anything—at the moment," he added. "If I took any sort of action the woman would stick to her tale. In the face of a string of darned lies I couldn't hope to make my story good. Even if I stood a chance of being believed I couldn't face it. She's a brazen cat and would swear anything. Nothing like this has ever happened to me before."

"I warned you about 'Stiff'."

"I know. But I didn't bargain he would employ a prize-fighter to do his dirty work. Lord, that woman could act. She looked as innocent as a new-born babe."

"Did you get her name?"

"No. She called the man Carl. That was the only name I heard. But one thing I did get—her handbag. She dropped it when she did that faked faint outside her door, and I slipped it into my pocket before I carried her in. I found it just now. That's it—on the table."

McLean took up the comparatively small handbag. He turned out the contents—a handkerchief, a few visiting cards bearing different names, a powder-puff and lipstick, and a wad of one-pound notes, in addition to some small change. McLean unfolded the notes, and uttered a low ejaculation as he held up one to the light.

" Got 'em ! "

" Got what ? "

" Our friends in carrying out that little job for ' Stiff ' have made a tremendous blunder. This is a batch of the dud notes. I'm willing to wager that ' Stiff ' is behind that counterfeit business, and that he paid the woman with some of the dud stuff for her part in the swindle. That was clever of ' Stiff,' but it is going to come back on him. You can now bear your aches and pains with complacency."

Brook grinned, but without any sign of complacency. It was the first time in his life that he had been knocked out, and the memory of it stung his pride.

" What are you going to do ? " he inquired.

" Visit your late friend and her prize-fighting husband. Tell me where I can find them."

" I'll come with you," said Brook. " I'm not so crocked up as all that."

Together they visited the scene of the previous

night's adventure, but the flat was empty, and the porter knew nothing of either the man or the woman. He stated that the apartment belonged to an elderly gentleman who was now in South Africa.

"The birds have flown," said McLean. "Either they had no intention of staying there, or the discovery of the loss of the handbag caused them to get out quick. We must look elsewhere, and the visiting cards may assist us."

§

The story of Brook's mauling had gone the rounds, and Brook found himself in an ignominious position. On every possible occasion he visited the gymnasium, and put in good time at the punching-ball and other aids to physical perfection.

"What the idea?" asked McLean.

"I'm just keeping fit," said Brook grimly. "One day I may meet friend Carl again."

"Isn't he a little above your class?"

"Well, yes. But I discovered one thing—when it was too late to take advantage of it. His jaw is like cast-iron, and he's got steel bands round his solar plexus, but tap him on the heart and he's gasping. I'm going to remember that."

McLean got busy with the visiting cards. They led him to all kinds of strange individuals, some of whom he knew to be crooks. Little by little information was gleaned. There was a woman named Natacha de Frece who answered exactly Brook's description. She was of mixed nationality, having had a French father and an English mother. Her adventurous life had been spent in various countries, including America. " Stiff " Colyer had mysteriously vanished, and Natacha was as difficult to locate as a needle in a hayrick.

Some days passed, and Brook's physical injuries healed, but the damage to his pride remained. As a rule he was a poor investigator, but when he really put his mind to it Brook could achieve wonders. He came to the office one morning with a smile of contentment on his face, and a cutting from an old sporting paper in his hand.

" Got him ! " he said.

" Got who ? "

" Carl—the bruiser. Here's a cutting from an American sporting journal—a year old. Carl Brun—German-American—won various heavy-weight contests, Arizona, Texas, Jersey City. Strained his heart in a fierce contest with Mahoney—advised to leave the ring. Just what I thought."

" Brook, you are improving," said McLean.

" Every day, in every way, I am getting better and better," quoted Brook, thumping himself on the chest. " Eight pounds off my weight. That's through giving up bacon and eggs for breakfast, and taking grape-fruit and dry toast. Any luck in your direction, Inspector ? "

" A little. I am meeting a certain person this evening who may tell me something about ' Stiff,' and probably Natacha. It is also possible we may find Carl."

" That sounds good," said Brook.

McLean's nocturnal mission was to a house of evil repute. He had long suspected the place as a " dope-shop " and rendezvous for crooks and other human blight, and when he was safely inside it he realised that his conclusions were correct. He was got up as a very " horsey " individual, with a loud suit and lank over-oiled hair. A wonderful Semitic accent and several flashy rings helped to make him the genuine article.

The place was full of " bullies," unfortunate women and decadent youths, and the atmosphere was poisonous. There was some dancing, a lot of drinking, and in a private room a small roulette wheel was at work. McLean marked the place down for a future raid, but at the moment his mission was different. Unable to find the person he sought among the dancers and drinkers, he wandered into the gaming-room, and there had better luck. Seated at the table near the croupier was a woman of about thirty-five, with a pile of counters before her. She had once been beautiful, but now her features had coarsened and her eyes were full of avarice. McLean soon saw that she was losing, and as there was a vacant seat beside her, he occupied it, and bought some counters from the croupier.

"Any luck, Rose?" he asked.

"Rotten! But who told you my name?"

"You've got a short memory. I met you once with a girl named Natacha."

"I don't remember."

"About two years ago. 'Stiff' was there too. You know 'Stiff'?"

"You bet. But I can't place you."

McLean laughed and backed a block of numbers somewhat heavily. He won and received quite a large pile of chips. Rose's eyes glistened, for her own capital was getting low.

"You've got luck," she said. "I can't get any."

"Try the black."

"Don't fancy it."

"I'll put a bit on for you. My luck's in."

He placed a fair stake on the black column, and it won.

"Yours," he said. "But let it stay."

She let the accumulating money stay three times, and then begged to be allowed to take it up. McLean agreed, and she clawed the pile of pieces.

"I'm through," she sighed. "Let's go and have a drink."

They left the gaming den, and Rose stood drinks in the larger room.

" Say, what is your name ? " she queried.

" Yales—Luke Yales. I do a bit with the ' gees.' That's how I got to know ' Stiff ' and Natacha. ' Stiff ' soaked me pretty well until he got put away."

" A bookmaker ? "

" At times."

" Well, you seem to do well out of it," she laughed, glancing at his rings. " You might let me in on a good thing."

" So I will. I'll put you a bit on a dark runner to-morrow. Leave it to me. If it comes down you can pay when you're flush. If it wins, I'll meet you here on Thursday same time, and pay up."

" You're a good sport."

McLean winked knowingly.

" I get some good information at times."

He was satisfied in merely scattering a few random seeds that evening. Naturally the " dark runner " won, and on Thursday evening McLean turned up at the house with six pounds for Rose. She insisted upon standing drinks, and after a while her tongue became very loose.

" Can't understand what ' Stiff ' and Natacha are doing," mused McLean. " Seem to have disappeared off the blooming earth."

" Aw, the cops got too busy when ' Stiff ' came

out. He simply had to lie low. I heard he had a dust-up with the fellow who put him away. But maybe it's only a rumour. Anyway I reckon I could put my hand on him."

"Wish *I* could. I got a bit of information to give him that might be useful. But there's only two days left. Guess I could make a couple of hundred out of it."

"One good turn deserves another," hiccoughed Rose. "You can get 'Stiff' any time at the 'White Horse' in Caledonian Road. Run by a fellow named Brun, but 'Stiff' lives there, and the best time to get him is after closing time. If you make your couple of hundred you can hand over a bit of commission, eh?"

"Sure I will."

Later he left Rose still spending her imaginary winnings, and went home feeling that the money had been well expended.

§

"Well, Brook, have you found your old friend Carl?" inquired McLean the next morning.

"Not yet. He's lying low."

"Would it interest you to know that I have?"

Brook's head came up.

"You—you mean that?"

"Yes—and 'Stiff.' Carl is running a low-class

'pub,' and 'Stiff' is his lodger. I am rather anxious to have a look into the cellars of that place, and I propose running along this evening—with you."

"Fine!"

"But before that I intend taking a morning *apéritif* there to see how the land lies. I'll see you before you go to lunch."

The public-house was of the lowest type, and chiefly frequented by men from the big market. McLean drifted into the evil-smelling bar, looking like a vendor of anything from meat to vegetables. He called for a drink, and became very interested in the barmaid. That she was Natacha he had no doubt at all, for Brun, who was on the premises, called her "Nat." It was satisfactory to find all the birds in one coop. McLean did not linger long there. He walked round the outside of the building and found that the cellar had a flap in the court behind down which supplies of drink were trundled. The flap was now closed and secured by a padlock. In addition there were undoubtedly two bolts inside. But the two sides of the wooden flap did not fit well, and it was possible for any intending burglar to sever them by working a thin hack-saw through the slits.

Shortly after ten o'clock that evening McLean and Brook sallied forth. When they reached the "White Horse" it was closed for the night, and there was but one light in the upper portion. The two officers went into the court at the back. It was a cul-de-sac and therefore unfrequented. McLean produced a hack-saw, and after oiling the blade got busy on the flap fastenings. There was scarcely any noise, and the well-tempered blade ate quickly through the ring of the padlock, and then the two bolts. Brook listened, with his ear to the flap.

"All quiet," he whispered.

"Then we'll go in. Lend me a hand."

The flap was raised, and they saw a wooden chute leading down. McLean flashed a torch and then they both entered, letting the flap down after them. Immediately below were many barrels of beer, and bins containing bottles. That compartment was innocent enough, and scant time was wasted on it. At the far end was a door. McLean made towards it, and found it locked and without a key.

"We'll try our little bunch of gadgets," he whispered.

He produced a number of queer crook's tools on a ring, and after trying one or two of them succeeded in opening the door. The torch revealed a small room with a domed ceiling. There was no window of any kind, and the only form of lighting was a paraffin lamp. In the far corner was a fairly large contraption covered by a cloth. McLean lifted the cloth and revealed a printing press.

"Got it!"

"And the plate?"

"Not here—at least, not in the press. There's a drawer and a cupboard!"

Both these were forced, and at last McLean found what he wanted—a well-engraved plate of a one-pound Treasury note. Also there were a number of faulty notes in a box. They bore the same number as the counterfeit notes found in Natacha's handbag.

"That's good enough," said McLean. "Now I think——"

He stopped suddenly as his keen ears heard a noise from without. The door opened abruptly and McLean's torch shone on the evil face of "Stiff" Colyer.

"What the h——! Carl!" he yelled.

"Get him, Brook!"

Brook leaped like a panther at his old enemy, but in a flash "Stiff" produced a revolver. The next instant there was a sharp report and a groan. "Stiff's" revolver fell to the floor and Stiff was nursing a wounded arm. McLean shrugged his shoulders as he looked at his smoking pistol.

"He'll be less dangerous now, Brook. Put the bracelets on."

Brook snapped on the handcuffs just as the half-closed door was pushed violently open, and Carl appeared. He had a pistol in his left hand. Brook swung round and grabbed the wrist which held it.

Carl went hurtling backward into the outer cellar, and Brook followed him. McLean picked up the fallen pistol and ran out.

"Hands up, Brun! I want you!"

Carl scrambled to his feet, his bullet head projected forward, and hands clenched. Brook looked at McLean appealingly.

"Give me a chance, Inspector," he grunted. "I've been waiting for this."

McLean hesitated and then gave way. Brook flung off his coat and advanced on Carl.

"Put them up! I owe you something."

Carl laughed scornfully, and then removed his coat. His first lightning blow caught Brook on the side of the head. It must have caused great pain, but Brook simply grunted. From the point of boxing the odds were on the younger man, but Brook knew the weak joint in his armour. He took two more blows in the head and one in the ribs, and then he landed just where he wanted to—a straight left-handed right over Carl's heart. The big man gasped, staggered and collapsed like a concertina.

"All square!" said Brook. "I'll give him the count. One—two—three——"

McLean ran forward and leaned over the prostrate man.

"Brook, I believe——"

"Ten!" said Brook. "He's all right. Look, he's coming round. I'll fix him up now."

Carl ultimately rose to his feet with his hands secured. He was yet suffering from the blow, but was obviously not seriously hurt. He glared at Brook.

"The next time——" he gasped.

"Why talk of the distant future?" said Brook. "Now for that charming wife of yours."

"Wife! She's not——"

Natacha suddenly appeared at the top of the stairs. McLean beckoned her and she came down. When she saw Brook her face went crimson and then pallid.

"How's your heart?" asked Brook.

She looked towards "Stiff" Colyer, who was standing in the background with contorted face.

"I—I—I was told to do it," she stammered. "'Stiff' compelled——"

"Yah, little rat!" snarled "Stiff." "Anyway, you got nothing against me. You can't prove anything."

McLean produced the engraved plate from his pocket, and also the bundle of half-printed notes.

"You'll find some little difficulty in explaining this," he mused. "Are you ready, Brook?"

A quarter of an hour later Scotland Yard's fastest car called, and the disconsolate trio were soon speeding westwards. McLean turned to Sergeant Brook, who was rubbing the side of his head.

"Hurt, Brook?"

"Hurt? Not likely. It's like a—a kiss. I've been dreaming of this for a fortnight. Now I'll be able to go back to the old bacon and eggs."

McLean laughed. It was certainly Brook's day out!

V

§

"MISSING. A reward of £100 will be paid to any person giving information as will lead to the whereabouts of Ralph Marston, who has been missing from his home since April 21st. Last seen wearing light grey overcoat over dark suit, felt hat—driving Sunbeam touring car, No. XB 10109. Height five feet eight inches, age 56. Apply 20 Exeter Gardens, S.W., or any police station."

For over a week this advertisement appeared in several London and provincial newspapers, and then ceased. No information of any kind was forthcoming, and it looked as if Marston and his car had disappeared into space.

McLean made inquiries at the house of the vanished man, and learned from his heart-broken wife that her husband had left home on the morning of April 21st in his car. He had taken a bag of golf clubs with him, but had not fixed his destination.

He was a member of two suburban clubs, and she concluded that he had gone to one of them. When he failed to return to dinner she telephoned both golf clubs, only to be informed that her husband had not been seen at either of them.

" What was your husband by profession ? "

" Nothing. He was retired, but he used to be connected with the Stock Exchange."

" Healthy ? "

" Very."

It was established that on the day when Marston left home the weather was unsettled. Half an hour later it commenced to rain, and continued showery all day. Here, in McLean's opinion, was a possible explanation of Marston's change of venue. He had probably given up the idea of golf and had gone elsewhere for some purpose. But where ?

Some days later a little information was forwarded by a hotel at Maidenhead. A man answering the description had stopped there at half-past twelve and had taken lunch. The garage man remembered the car quite well. At any rate he was sure of the initial letters of the vehicle. To prove it he mentioned that the car was most difficult to start, owing to the battery having run down. It had been necessary to use the handle, and the engine was heavy and stiff.

These facts were borne out by Marston's chauffeur, who on that day had taken a holiday. At a quarter to two Marston had left the garage, but the man in charge could not say what direction he took. There the trail ended.

A month passed, and then a discovery was made by an angler who was fishing for eels in a very deep quarry pool in Berkshire. His hook became fouled, and he tugged hard on the line. Ultimately the hook was freed, and twisted around it was a small piece of grey cloth. He went at once to the local police, and McLean was communicated with.

On the following day the deep pool was dragged, and within an hour the dead body of Ralph Marston lay in the punt. The back of his skull was shattered, and there were small wounds down as far as the shoulder-blades.

" Shot-gun ! " mused McLean.

To ensure immersion in the water the pockets of the overcoat had been filled with large stones. The body was taken to the mortuary, and McLean resumed his investigations there. The doctor stated that death must have been instantaneous, for many of the small round shot had reached the brain, and the spinal cord was severed.

In all McLean recovered fifty-three shots, and from their close distribution he calculated that the murderer had fired the gun at a distance of no more than six yards. The various pockets contained few things—a pipe, tobacco pouch, matches, money and a few letters bearing no relation to the crime, so far as could be ascertained at the moment.

" Now for the car ! "

On examining the sides of the quarry McLean came to the conclusion that only in one place could a car be driven to the edge of the rock wall which enclosed the pool. A search was made at that point and the car was located deep down in the stagnant water. A derrick was rigged up, and twenty-four hours later a slime-coated Sunbeam car was hoisted out. It was towed into the nearest town.

One fact McLean noted. When the car was hoisted out the gear lever was in bottom gear. This agreed with other facts which he had observed. There was a steep rise from the moorland to the edge of the pool. The big car could not possibly be pushed. It was necessary for the murderer to enter it, set it moving and then jump out ere it took the plunge.

McLean examined the vehicle. There were a few perforations in the bonnet where some of the stray shots had penetrated. They proved that the dead man had been standing between the car and his murderer. Moreover, they were so low down that it looked as if the man who fired them had been standing on a higher elevation than his victim. It was at the end of his investigation that McLean came upon an object of extreme value. It was lying in the bottom of the car near the accelerator pedal—a rough leather button!

Another visit to the scene of the crime helped to reconstruct the murder. The main road ran about a hundred yards from the pool, and on both sides were fairly high banks. A man concealed behind one of the banks—probably the one furthest away from the car—would have caused just such a distribution of shots as had been found. McLean set the local police hunting for a possible empty cartridge case. Also he sent for Sergeant Brook, who was exceptionally good at finding things.

But neither Brook nor the local men had any luck on this occasion. All they did find on the site where McLean was convinced the shooting took place was an empty match-box of curious brand. It was, of course, extremely likely that this had been left by an ordinary innocent tourist, but McLean retained it.

"How did the murderer get the car to the pool?" asked Brook. "There seems to be no break in the bank."

"There is—half a mile further back."

"Then it looks like being someone who knew the district. No ordinary traveller would know there was a pool handy."

"No ordinary traveller would carry a shot-gun about with him," rejoined McLean dryly.

" And Marston was shot out of the car ? "

" Undoubtedly. I deduce he was in the act of starting it—with the handle—when his murderer appeared."

" Why did he leave the car here ? "

" Because it was the nearest point to some place of call. He paid a visit to someone, and having transacted his business—social or otherwise—he came back here to enter his car. He was followed and shot. All very simple. The difficult point is to discover exactly where he went. That is our next job."

There were half a dozen farms and habitations lying to the north of the moorland road. Three of these had possible means of approach by car, and McLean was inclined to rule these out, for it was improbable that the dead man would leave his car where he had if he could have driven to the door of his objective. That theory was not absolutely flawless, but it sufficed for the moment.

Subsequent inquiries produced nothing of value. None of the occupants of the neighbouring houses and farms knew anything about Marston, but a farm hand had seen the car standing on the road unattended at about four o'clock in the afternoon of the day in question.

" Where were you ? " asked McLean.

" I was walking into town, zur."

" You came back that afternoon ? "

" Aye—about six o'clock."

" The car was gone then ? "

" Aye, zur."

It helped to fix the time of the murder—but that was all. The nearest resident to the spot where the car had been left was an old man named James Geery. He lived by himself and ran a small holding. Conversation was difficult with him, as he was very deaf.

" Do you know a man named Marston ? " asked McLean.

" Carstone ? No, I've——"

" Not Carstone—Marston—Mr. Ralph Marston?"

" Never heard the name. I'm sure he doesn't live anywhere around here."

" I know that. Mr. Marston is the man whose body was found in the quarry pool."

Geery opened his eyes wide.

" The man with the car ? "

" Yes. I am under the impression he came to this district to call on someone. You are sure you have never heard that name ? "

" Quite sure. I don't have folks calling in big cars. Maybe Mr. Swaine at Upper Hennock will know——"

" Mr. Swaine knows nothing."

" He's the only man around here who would know folks who run big cars."

" You live here all alone ? "

"Yes—ever since my boy ran off to sea—three year ago. He used to help me, but he always had a hankering for the sea. I don't blame him either. A dull life for a young fellow in these parts. Was that gentleman killed and robbed?"

"He was killed, but not robbed."

"Must have been a stranger. Who would want to shoot a man in the back?"

"Someone certainly had a reason for wanting to do so. Is there much shooting going on round here?"

"Shooting!"

"Game shooting?"

"Little enough game. There's a few hares, but most folk carry a gun for rabbits. We're plagued with them creatures."

"Is that your gun in the corner?"

"Aye. I get a rabbit for the pot fairly often. As for rats—I've lost two fowls this last week——"

Rats seemed to be his bugbear, and he started to tell McLean of the various plans he had for exterminating the vermin. But McLean wasn't interested.

"What a life!" mused Brook, as he and McLean left the place. "Anyway he knows nothing."

§

Further investigations in the neighbourhood were unproductive, yet McLean was convinced that someone was lying. The shots taken from the dead man did not help, and it was doubtful whether the recovery of the cartridge case would have shed any light on the identity of the murderer, for nearly all the local farmers used the same brand of cartridge, purchased from the one and only gun-shop in the neighbouring town. A new line of investigation was opened at the home of Marston.

" Do you know of any business that might have taken your husband to that neighbourhood ? " inquired McLean of the heart-broken widow.

" No. My husband seldom mentioned any business matters to me."

" Had he any friends or acquaintances near where his body was found ? "

" I think not."

" You have no idea what induced him to change his mind about playing golf and drive into Berkshire ? "

" None at all."

" Did he receive any letters on that morning ? "

" I can't remember. He came down to breakfast before me, and any letters would be left on the table for him."

" By whom ? "

" The maid."

The maid was called. She remembered the morning in question. There had been two letters for her master, and she had left them beside his plate on the breakfast-table. One was from an insurance company, but the other was in a plain envelope.

" You are sure about this ? "

" Quite sure, sir."

Among the few things found on the dead man was a letter from an insurance company in regard to certain bonuses which had been declared. The other letters were documents which had obviously been contained in foolscap envelopes.

" What shape was the second letter—the plain one ? " asked McLean.

" The ordinary shape, sir."

" Not long—like this ? "

" Oh no, sir. Just the ordinary shape like every-one uses, and the writing was bad."

The chauffeur was then questioned. He had never on any occasion driven his master to the neighbourhood where his body was found. He knew that his master intended to play golf on that day, because he had been told so when he begged the day off to attend his sister's wedding. He himself had put the bag of clubs into the car on the day previous, at his master's request.

McLean dismissed him, and decided to investigate the matter of the missing letter. There were three possibilities. It might have been destroyed by Marston. It might still be among Marston's papers. It might have been found on Marston by his murderer, and destroyed by him because it contained matter that might be used as a clue. He begged access to Marston's private papers, and ultimately called on the family solicitor, who produced a big bundle of documents and letters. Many of them were share certificates in prosperous companies. Others were letters in connection with business—loans and mortgages—but none of them had any reference to Berkshire.

"You are searching for something?" inquired the solicitor.

"Yes—a letter that came to Marston on the morning of the day he was murdered. It may be here. But if it is, then it has no bearing upon the crime, but I rather fancy it is not any of these letters."

"These are all the documents that have been found."

"He kept them himself?"

"Yes. There was no need for the bank to hold them, for he always had a good cash balance there."

"He was wealthy?"

"Moderately so."

"He did not consult you with regard to his investments?"

"Oh no. He prided himself upon his business acumen and did everything himself."

McLean was temporarily baffled, and chiefly through the dead man's custom of keeping his business affairs strictly private. Why had he gone into Berkshire on that day? Had the missing letter reference to some business there, and he had gone when he found the weather unsuitable for golf? Or he might have planned to go there in any case—after his round of golf!

The complete absence of motive made the mystery almost impossible of solution. McLean could prove that the considerable sum of money found on the corpse was about what it should have been, and there was the gold watch—worth at least twenty pounds. Again McLean went into Berkshire. Fresh inquiries were started, and one afternoon he found something that aroused the first gleam of hope. He was walking down the path which led from the main road to old Geery's house, when he found a small wax match. Later he found another, nearer the house. The matches were peculiar—smaller than those which were normally offered for sale in England. When he compared them with the box which he had previously found, they fitted the narrow width exactly. The box was of Italian make, working on two thin pieces of elastic.

He investigated the ground all round the house, and in two hours he found the remains of five more wax matches. The box had been found near the spot where he was convinced the shooting had taken place, and the matches near Geery's house. These facts were too significant to be disregarded.

Later came Geery from the direction of his hen-coops. He looked astonished to see McLean, but managed to smile. McLean produced a cigarette, and hunted for matches—in vain.

"Do you happen to have a light?" he begged.

Geery slapped his coat.

"Indoors," he said. "I don't smoke often."

McLean entered the house, and Geery found a box of matches, but they were common wooden matches.

"Any news about the murder?" asked Geery.

"Oh yes, we've got the fellow."

"What!"

"That's private and confidential."

Geery blinked in a strange manner. McLean let the cigarette go out and then, thoughtlessly, produced the empty box found on the scene of the crime. He saw Geery's eyes switch to it.

"Ah, empty!" he said. "Have you ever seen this brand before?"

Geery gulped and shook his head.

"You have," said McLean. "They were once in this house."

"That's not true——"

McLean suddenly turned and locked the door, pocketing the key. Geery started and placed his hand over his heart.

" What's—what's——? "

" I am going to search this house, and you are going to help me. Come—the key of that cupboard ! "

The cupboard was opened, but it contained nothing of value to McLean. They went from room to room, until they reached the small back bedroom. Here in a corner cupboard McLean found an old short coat. It had leather buttons down the front and on the sleeves. Those down the front were intact, but from the right sleeve a button was missing.

" Is this your coat ? "

" Aye, but what——? "

McLean produced the missing button from his pocket. He compared it with those on the coat, and found it was exactly similar.

" I am going to arrest you, Mr. Geery," he said.

" Eh ! "

" This button—from your coat—was found on the floor of the murdered man's car. I must warn you that anything you——"

Geery's face went green. He said something unintelligible, and then suddenly collapsed. McLean brought him round with some difficulty and then took him away.

§

Three days later Geery was charged with murder and committed for trial. The evidence against him was strong, but the motive was yet absent.

"Fancy it being him!" said Brook. "Why, he didn't look strong enough to kill a cat!"

"He hasn't been found guilty yet," warned McLean.

"But the button, and the match-box!"

"There is still a great deal to come out."

On the following day a lot did come out. Geery said he wished to make a statement, and it was taken down. It was a full confession and gave the motive. For years Geery had been living from hand to mouth. He had borrowed money against the security of his freehold from Marston, to whom he was introduced by another farmer. Marston had extorted a high rate of interest, until at last the old man saw ruin staring him in the face. Marston had pressed for payment of the capital and threatened to foreclose. Geery had begged him to wait, as he expected a legacy at any moment. But when it was near the day of foreclosure Geery thought of a grim plan to free himself. He wrote to Marston and told him that he had now received the legacy. If he would come down he would hand him the money in exchange for the deeds. Marston called at half-past four in the afternoon.

Geery's courage had failed him in the house, and he had to admit that the money had not arrived. Marston was furious and told him that he would foreclose on the morrow. He left, but immediately Geery had a reaction. He took his shot-gun and followed Marston. Then taking a short cut he concealed himself behind the bank that fringed the road. Marston arrived a few minutes later. He went to start the engine and Geery shot him. Afterwards he put the body in the car, drove it along the road until he found a break in the banking. Here he drove the car on to the moorland, and made for the deep pool. The rest bore out what had been discovered.

"And that's that," said Brook. "But for the button he might have got away with it."

McLean shrugged his shoulders in a strange way.

"Have you seen that car, Brook?" he asked.

"Yes."

"Have you tried to start it by the handle?"

"Start it!"

"Well, I have, and it nearly killed me. Oh no, Brook. We aren't finished yet. In a few days we shall have a little more light on the subject."

"But the statement?"

"True up to a point. But nothing in this world will induce me to believe that Geery started that car, drove it to the edge of the pool, flung his victim into the water, and then started the car again and leapt out of it while it was moving."

" But why should he say so ? "

" Because he has but a short time to live. We have it on medical evidence that he is suffering from advanced heart disease. He knows he is doomed in any case. To-morrow you and I are going to Southampton."

At Southampton McLean and Brook were compelled to wait two days, for the S.S. *Ramola* had encountered bad weather in the Bay of Biscay and was late. At last she arrived in port—a dirty little tramp steamer carrying wine and other produce from Genoa. McLean and Brook boarded the ship as she berthed, and McLean at once interrogated the captain. As a result a deck-hand was called. He was a well-built man of about thirty—a determined-looking fellow.

" Your name is Geery ? "

" That's so."

" I want to know where you were on April 21st last ? "

" April 21st ? You can't expect me to remember——"

" I do. It isn't a difficult matter. On April 18th your ship berthed here. What did you do afterwards ? "

" I—I went to London."

" Go on."

"And stayed there until the ship sailed again on April 23rd."

"You did nothing of the kind," retorted McLean. "You went home to your father in Berkshire, and you stayed there until after April 21st. I have here a letter from you, written from Genoa, informing your father of the date of your arrival. Also a telegram from this port. Do you admit writing those?"

"Yes. But I never went home."

"Can you prove that?"

Geery's face became contorted.

"Can you prove I did go home?" he asked.

"Yes. On April 20th you wrote a letter to a Mr. Marston, inviting him to call on a certain matter of business."

"It's a lie."

"And he called. Your father was out, but you were in. Marston expected to see your father, but he was not there. You had some words with him, and ultimately he left in a temper. You followed him to his car, and you took a shot-gun——"

"It's a lie!"

"I am going to arrest you for the murder of Ralph Marston."

"It is not true."

They took him along with them. He was charged with complicity, and he awaited his trial in a stubborn frame of mind. One day McLean walked into his cell.

"Your father was tried to-day," he said.

The prisoner's face went pallid.

"My father! Tried? For what?"

"Murder."

"Great God! You never told me. I didn't know. Has he—he hasn't been found—guilty?"

"He confessed."

An agonised expression passed over Geery's face. He beat his broad chest with his hands and then sank down on his bed, the picture of dejection. McLean left him, but two hours later he was told that Geery wished to see him. He re-entered the cell. Geery was pacing to and fro. He stopped dead as he heard the door open.

"My father—is he well?"

"Bearing up."

"You're not lying to me? He did confess?"

"I have here a copy of his statement. Read it!"

The prisoner took the document with trembling hands. He perused it and then tore it to shreds.

"He's not going to suffer for me," he said thickly. "He never did that. I did it. He told me about that—that swine. For years and years he had been paying high interest. I wanted the last year or so of his life to be happy. I wrote to Marston in my father's name, and managed to get my father out of the farm for the day. I knew the pool—and had already planned to sink him in that. I did it. My father came home and found blood on my hands. I—I had to tell him. I was going to give myself up, but he begged me not to."

"And the letter you wrote to him. You got that?"

"Yes. It was in his pocket with the deeds. I took it—and the deeds. I'll tell you anything you want to know. But let me see the old man—that's all I ask."

McLean was not present at that meeting. It was one of the many painful cases in which he had figured.

McLEAN INVESTIGATES   VI

§

WHENEVER Brook lounged into the office with his hands thrust deep into his trousers pockets, and his big face as seraphic as any angel's, it was a sure sign to McLean that his subordinate had discovered some fact of minor or major importance—usually minor, for Sergeant Brook, excellent as he was in rough work, was not by nature suitable for the more subtle jobs.

"How now, Brook," he said, without looking up. "What is the latest scandal in crook circles?"

"Gertie the Red is in London."

"Any objections?"

"Lots. I thought you would be interested to

know. We haven't heard much of her since the Paris affair."

"Where did you see her?"

"Benthams. I went there to have a meal, and there was Gertie, looking as fine as ever, sharing a bottle of fizz with a dark fellow who looked like an Italian."

"Did she see you?"

"She did. When I was leaving she kissed her hand to me."

"Ah, now I divine the cause of your obvious elation. A kiss from Gertie is as rare as the V.C. Anything more?"

"A little. Naturally I hung around, and in about half an hour Gertie and her pal came out. They went to the car-park in the square and drove off in the biggest car I've ever seen. I took the number—a French one."

"Splendid! You can devote the rest of the day to tracing the owner of the car. When Gertie comes to town, strange things have a way of happening. Wonderful woman that!"

So far McLean had never come into actual contact with Gertie. But he knew enough about her to be able to write her biography. Her history was one long series of adventures, and she managed to steer her way through the police net with the dexterity of a weasel. Her sobriquet was based on her appearance, for she possessed a marvellous head of bright auburn hair, which on occasion she concealed with great cunning. She was big and muscular, and could pose as a man with considerable success. Only once had she been charged, and on that occasion she managed to prove an alibi.

The police from Edinburgh to Scotland Yard knew perfectly well that the celebrated adventuress figured in many a startling crime, but to prove it was a matter of the utmost difficulty. She had been everything, from an artist's model to a cabaret dancer, and she knew the ways of the world as well as its oldest inhabitant. McLean had left her alone because she had never really come into his sphere of action, but now things were comparatively quiet and he experienced the desire to curtail the activities of Gertie.

By the next morning Brook had managed to get details as to the owner of the big car. He was Pietro Tamargo, an Italian, but resident in Paris, and the car had been first licensed three months before—a fifty horse-power Renault Saloon.

"If he's known to the Paris police it won't be under that name," said McLean. "We'll see what information they have."

A telephone call was put through to Paris, and later in the day some important information arrived. Tamargo was an old offender under various aliases. He had figured prominently in some big financial swindles both in Rome and Paris, and had served two sentences—one for embezzlement and the other for larceny. In his youth he had been an actor. In all he was a man of many parts.

"A nice sort of combination," mused McLean. "With Tamargo's genius added to Gertie's wits we ought to see some interesting developments. We must keep in touch with them."

Some weeks passed and nothing more was seen of Gertie, but in the meantime McLean had discovered the address of Tamargo. He was living in a small but good-class hotel off Berkeley Square, and his car was garaged close by. Gertie seemed to have disappeared, for Tamargo was shadowed to innumerable places, in none of which was there any likelihood of Gertie being present.

At last came news of Gertie. McLean learned that she was crossing from France to England by the afternoon boat. At about six o'clock he went to Victoria Station and waited for the continental train to arrive. Gertie sailed along the platform in due course and hired a taxi. McLean followed her example and kept on her trail until she alighted at a flat in Kensington. That evening McLean dined in a restaurant fairly close to Gertie and her friend Tamargo, but strain his ears as he might he was unable to overhear any of their tense conversation. That something big was being planned he had no doubt, and he resolved to watch every movement of the pair of conspirators.

On the following morning Gertie left her flat soon after ten o'clock and took a taxi to a registry office in Bond Street. McLean, attired like a very respectable country parson, entered the office after her. While Gertie was being attended to by the manageress, another member of the agency came to McLean. He said he urgently required a cook at his vicarage in the country. Had they any domestics on their books? While he was giving details of wages, etc., his ears were alert to discover Gertie's requirements. She was in need of a maid—a French girl if possible. She considered them more reliable. Knowledge of English did not matter. In fact she preferred to speak French to the girl. Wages— she would pay good wages.

McLean knew that his cook for an isolated vicarage in the country would not materialise at the wages he offered, and since the said vicarage never had an existence in fact, it was as well there were no applicants. But Gertie's requirements interested him, and late that afternoon he was interviewing a charming young woman who on many occasions had worked for the C.I.D. She was named Madeline, and could speak fluently five European languages. In addition she had great intelligence, and never missed any point that was of the slightest value.

"I want you to get that post," said McLean. "Just drop in casually and plead an absolute ignorance of English. I fancy Gertie would prefer that. You can produce references if she asks for them?"

Madeline's eyes twinkled, for she was well armed with credentials of every conceivable kind.

" How shall I report to you?" she inquired.

" At my private number each evening at seven o'clock. If I have occasion to telephone you I will give the name of Alphonse. You had better make the way clear for that by passing off Alphonse as your brother. But the first thing is to get the post. I leave that to your powers of fascination."

Madeline went off at once, made herself up in decided Parisian style, and then dropped in on the agent. She had a brother in London and wished to find a post in order to be near him, also to learn English. Would m'sieur do what he could for her?

M'sieur wrestled with his French. By a coincidence he had an inquiry for a lady's-maid—preferably French. He might be able to arrange an interview at once. Would Mademoiselle wait while he telephoned? The upshot was that Gertie was willing to see the applicant immediately, and Madeline was soon inside Gertie's flat. Gertie's rather cold eyes roved over the very attractive form.

" You are French?"

" Oui, Madame."

" You have had experience as a lady's-maid?"

"In Paris, Madame, but not in England. I came to London to be near my brother, Alphonse. He is in a hotel. If Madame requires testimonials —— ? "

Madame did not. She was accustomed to judging people by their faces, and Madeline could have passed any tribunal. She looked simple—yet capable. She was neat in her dress and in her person. Gertie inclined her head.

"I will give you a trial provided you can start to-morrow. Is that convenient?"

It was. Madeline promised to bring her box along at eight o'clock the following morning. That evening McLean heard that all had gone well—so far. At nine o'clock the next morning Madeline was dealing with her mistress's mop of auburn hair in expert style.

"Madame has a wonderful head of hair," she said.

Gertie laughed, not displeased with the compliment.

"It has got me into enough trouble," she said. "Red hair is to men what nectar is to bees. The fools!"

"Madame does not like the men?"

"Not much. There are no really good specimens of that sex. Some are not quite so impossible as others. That is the best one can say about them."

Madeline seemed to be incurably French. Gertie,

who knew Paris like her two hands, recognised various little traits that seemed to stamp her new maid as the genuine article. Once or twice she tried her with a sudden remark in English, only to be met with an uncomprehending stare.

"I regret, Madame."

"Oh, I forgot. You must learn English, Madeline."

"I will try, but it is very difficult."

Three days passed, and then Madeline saw McLean in person. They met by appointment in a café near Oxford Circus—McLean impersonating the imaginary Alphonse in case of accidents.

"Any news?" he asked.

"A little. Tamargo called last night—after I telephoned you. He and Gertie had a meal at home. The cook had gone out, so it was an excellent chance for me to take her place. I dished them up some soup and an omelette. I overheard one or two remarks. It looks as if Tamargo is in the film business. He mentioned cameras and 'shooting,' which I took to be a movie term. Apparently Gertie is to be starred."

McLean wrinkled his brows at this.

"Where's the studio?"

"I don't know. I heard two names mentioned. One was Dugard and the other Weininger."

"In what connection?"

"That is indefinite. Tamargo said, 'Dugard

will manage that business. He used to produce for the Sphinx Company.'"

"Has Gertie said anything about this film work?"

"Not a word. But I shall put a leading question at a favourable opportunity. One thing is clear—Tamargo isn't in love with her. The only relationship that exists between them is a business one. She treats all men with contempt."

"Can you manage to get anything out of Tamargo?"

"It may be possible. He seemed interested in me."

"I can understand that."

"If he invites me out to dinner I shall go."

"Do. But let me know if that should take place. In the meantime, try to find out who Dugard and Weininger are."

§

Gertie the Red and her companion in crime—Tamargo—were dining in style at the best and most exclusive restaurant in London. Few people would have taken them to be anything else but well-to-do members of society, for both were perfectly turned out, and conducted themselves faultlessly. Gertie's red hair was more arrestive than ever this evening, for Madeline's clever hands had put the finishing touches to it.

in a stubborn frame of mind. One day McLean walked into his cell.

"Your father was tried to-day," he said.

The prisoner's face went pallid.

"My father! Tried? For what?"

"Murder."

"Great God! You never told me. I didn't know. Has he—he hasn't been found—guilty?"

"He confessed."

An agonised expression passed over Geery's face. He beat his broad chest with his hands and then sank down on his bed, the picture of dejection. McLean left him, but two hours later he was told that Geery wished to see him. He re-entered the cell. Geery was pacing to and fro. He stopped dead as he heard the door open.

"My father—is he well?"

"Bearing up."

"You're not lying to me? He did confess?"

"I have here a copy of his statement. Read it!"

The prisoner took the document with trembling hands. He perused it and then tore it to shreds.

"He's not going to suffer for me," he said thickly. "He never did that. I did it. He told me about that—that swine. For years and years he had been paying high interest. I wanted the last year or so of his life to be happy. I wrote to Marston in my father's name, and managed to get my father out of the farm for the day. I knew the pool—and had already planned to sink him in that. I did it. My father came home and found blood on my hands. I—I had to tell him. I was going to give myself up, but he begged me not to."

" And the letter you wrote to him. You got that ? "

" Yes. It was in his pocket with the deeds. I took it—and the deeds. I'll tell you anything you want to know. But let me see the old man—that's all I ask."

McLean was not present at that meeting. It was one of the many painful cases in which he had figured.

VI

Whenever Brook lounged into the office with his hands thrust deep into his trousers pockets, and his big face as seraphic as any angel's, it was a sure sign to McLean that his subordinate had discovered some fact of minor or major importance—usually minor, for Sergeant Brook, excellent as he was in rough work, was not by nature suitable for the more subtle jobs.

" How now, Brook," he said, without looking up. " What is the latest scandal in crook circles ? "

" Gertie the Red is in London."

" Any objections ? "

" Lots. I thought you would be interested to

She hesitated, and then shook her head. But Tamargo did not accept that as final.

"Think it over," he begged. "You are lonely, and so am I. Anyway, I will wait for you."

She shot him a sly glance as Gertie reappeared and put an end to the conversation. Tamargo congratulated himself. Of course she would·be there. He knew these French girls! McLean was duly informed of the rendezvous, and approved of it.

"I can't get anything definite about the man Dugard, nor Weininger," he said. "See what you can worm out of him. Anyway, I shall not be far off."

Madeline kept the appointment, and McLean followed them to a restaurant. He entered the cloak-room hot on Tamargo's heels and managed to get his coat hung quite close to Tamargo's. While the attendant was not looking he changed over the numbers. Some time later he called for his overcoat and was given Tamargo's. The ruse served him rather well, for in the inside pocket were several letters. He slipped these into his inner pocket and then complained that he had been given the wrong coat. There was some altercation, but he proved that the adjacent coat was his by comparing his visiting card with a letter which he had purposely left in the pocket of his overcoat.

Later he perused the letters which he had taken

from Tamargo's coat. Several of them were of no importance whatever, but there was one signed by Georges Dugard.

"Dear Pietro,
"I have now completed my arrangements. Will be at the corner of George Street at six a.m. as instructed. My men are absolutely reliable, and I have managed to get the necessary uniforms—three constables and a sergeant. I understand that you will bring the gear and the other persons.
"Yours in haste."

McLean was disappointed at the absence of any address on the letter. It left Dugard in the air, so to speak. Obviously a robbery of some kind was planned at a certain address on an unknown day. The only thing certain was the time, six o'clock in the morning! That was a little surprising, for at that time of the day it was broad daylight. As for the meeting-place—George Street, there were dozens of George Streets in London. The only other clue at the moment was the name Weininger. Who was Weininger?

§

On the following day he saw Madeline. She had had a hectic time with Tamargo. Her evening out had ended at nearly two o'clock in the morning, by which time Tamargo was well on the way to intoxication. He had made violent love to her, and she had encouraged him up to a point.

" Did you get anything out of him ? "

" Not directly. But he hinted that he was going abroad soon, and that he and I might meet in Paris. I had told him that I was keen to get on to the films, and he swore he could help me. I told him I would think it over and tell him next Tuesday. But Tuesday would not suit him, from which I concluded he would not be in London on that day. Then I tried Monday, but Monday was also inconvenient. We compromised on Saturday."

" That looks as if the job was planned for Sunday or Monday morning ? "

" Why the morning ? "

" I have established that fact. Now I want Dugard's address. At the first opportunity you will tell Gertie that a man rang up who gave a name that you did not hear distinctly. Suggest Dugard —anything that bears a close resemblance. Say that he requested her to telephone him as soon as possible, and then try to find out his number."

This ruse was carried out later in the day. By good luck Dugard was not in, so Gertie was not in the least suspicious. Madeline immediately telephoned the number to McLean, and Dugard was rendered less nebulous. For twenty-four hours

McLean and Brook were exceedingly busy, and at last the various pieces of the puzzle were fitted together. While McLean had devoted his attention to Dugard, Brook had been looking up a number of George Streets, and reporting upon their locality and so forth. It was George Street off Portman Square that met with all requirements, for within a hundred yards of it was the house of Aldous Weininger—dealer in gems and other things.

"There is no other Weininger anywhere near a George Street," asserted Brook. "But it isn't a certainty that Weininger's is the prospective job."

"Nothing is a certainty in this life. But the combination of Weininger, George Street, and precious gems cannot be overlooked. Last night I saw Dugard and three of his cronies. I overheard but a few words. They were sufficient to let in a lot of light. On Sunday morning we are going to get Gertie and her friend Tamargo, and quite a number of other crooked people. The plot is rather neat—one of those very bold and spectacular things that sometimes come off."

"Where does Gertie come in?"

"Gertie? Why she is the star turn. I shall need you, Brook, and two constables. I personally am going in for an Irishman's rise—to the extent of being reduced to a plain 'bobby.'"

At six o'clock on Sunday morning George Street

and its neighbourhood was as quiet as a cemetery. At five minutes past six the policeman on his beat saw two cars arrive, both bearing the name of a very well-known Film-producing Company. One of these contained men with photographic apparatus, and the other three men and a woman in vivid make-up. The woman was Gertie, and her complexion was a sickly mixture of green and yellow paint. Tamargo wore a slouch hat and a villainous moustache, while two other men were obviously intended to be (and really were) crooks. With them was Dugard, armed with an enormous megaphone. The constable on point duty loitered, and watched the subsequent proceedings.

Two cameras were erected opposite Weininger's premises, and Dugard began to bawl his instructions. Gertie was to enter the shop. She was to answer the door to the crooks, who would overpower her. But while they were rifling the safe she would escape, run to the window on the first floor and blow a policeman's whistle. Higher up the street was a car containing four officers of the law. They would start their car just after the crooks left the premises, but would give them time to get away. After that a chase would commence.

"Have you got that, Denny?" bawled Dugard to the policeman at the wheel of the waiting car.

"Sure!"

"Good! Now Miss Goodfellow!"

This to Gertie, who was calmly smoking a cigarette. She flung away the stump and accompanied Dugard and another man to the door of the shop. Dugard rang the bell, and after a few seconds' wait the night watchman answered the summons. He stared hard at the visitors and then at the men in the street who were operating their cameras.

"What do you——?" he commenced.

Dugard and his male companion sprang at him. A saturated pad was clapped over his nose, and in a few seconds he was unconscious. They bore him to a small room behind the shop, disarmed him and locked the door on him.

"He won't hurt for half an hour," grunted Dugard. "Now we'll start the play. Stay here, but answer the door when we knock."

Dugard and his companion emerged. The vital part of the show now started. The band of crooks approached the door while the camera clicked. They knocked and Gertie answered it. The policeman had now moved closer in order not to miss the fun. He saw Gertie man-handled and the door closed. Dugard mopped his brow and stopped the camera.

"We'll now shoot the window scene," he said.

The camera was moved, and there was considerable delay, in order to give the crooks time to open the safe. Dugard got into conversation with the policeman.

"Not likely to be any traffic for half an hour, is there?"

"Not at this hour of the morning—and on Sunday."

"Good!"

"What is it—crook film?"

"Yes."

There was a cry from the window and Gertie's head appeared.

"Are you ready for me?" she asked.

"In a minute. Have you got the whistle?"

"Yes."

"I'll give you the cue." He turned to the man with the camera, and squinted up at the window. "That's all right."

Followed the "shooting." That bit was done four times, for the safe-crackers were not yet ready. Then Gertie gave an arranged signal, and Dugard turned his attention to the shop door. It opened and his band of confederates were seen, all looking somewhat anxious. Again the camera was moved.

"Supposed to have robbed the safe?" queried the constable.

"Yes. Pockets full of jewels. Now, Bill—hold that expression. You have just seen the cops coming. Good! Make for the big car as hard as you can go——"

At that moment something went wrong. Dugard turned his head and saw the police car moving towards him.

"Get back, you idiots!" he bawled. "Not yet. I'll give you your cue. Do you want to spoil the whole picture?"

But the car came on until its front wheels prevented both the waiting cars from moving. Tamargo, who was at the steering wheel of the Renault, began to curse. Dugard stopped the camera man and turned angrily on the policeman.

"Who told you to butt in like——?"

He stopped and gasped. The four stalwart officers had their faces made-up *à la* cinema, but he failed to recognise any of them.

"Denny!" he gasped. "Where's Denny?"

Sergeant Brook laughed, and suddenly blew a whistle. A big closed van appeared at the other end of the short street, and from its interior emerged more policemen.

"Trapped!" ejaculated Tamargo.

McLean in the guise of an ordinary constable went across to the shop door. Gertie emerged as he reached it, and stood transfixed to observe all the members of her party in custody.

"What does this mean, constable?" she blustered.

"Just a little respite from film acting," replied McLean. "A very strenuous profession at the best of times. I had no idea that Gertie the Red had turned film star. Brook, take charge of this lady. I rather imagine the night watchman requires some attention."

While McLean brought the night watchman to his senses, the policeman on point duty stole away —a sadder and wiser man. On the following day the magistrate was exceedingly busy.

"What a job they made of that safe," mused Brook. "They went through it like cheese."

"Yes. There is nothing like sticking to one's profession. They were first-class cracksmen, but bum actors."

That evening he and the fair Madeline had a little meal together to celebrate a record haul, while Gertie the Red remained ignorant of the means by which her cherished freedom had been so suddenly and cruelly curtailed.

McLEAN INVESTIGATES VII

§

As a general rule McLean's successes were gained by sheer brain work, patience, and a wide knowledge of human nature. But there were occasions when the element of luck crept in, and in no case did it serve him better than in that of Mrs. Laverton.

McLean was working late at the office when a

telephone call came from a house in High Barnet. It was the maid speaking, and she averred that she had returned home after her " evening out " to find her mistress lying on the drawing-room couch —dead. The voice was high-pitched and near to breaking point. McLean asked the cause of death, but got no satisfactory reply. He thereupon promised to call immediately.

Ten minutes later he and a police surgeon, named Gines, were making towards High Barnet in a fast car. Ultimately they reached the house— a quite modest residence on the corner of a street. A girl answered the door, and it was easy to know that she was the person who had used the telephone, for the voice was unique.

" You—you are from Scotland Yard ? " she quavered.

" Yes. We should like to see the deceased."

She gulped and led them to a large room which overlooked a small lawn. It was well furnished— chiefly antiques. On the left was a grand piano, and close to it a big wireless set. On the right was a couch, beside which was a low brass table of Eastern design, bearing a carafe half full of water, and a glass. In the centre of the room was a small octagonal table carrying a flowering plant in a lovely porcelain pot. The woman lay on the couch in a reposeful position. The eyes were closed and the face pallid. She was middle-aged, with good features and abundant iron-grey hair, and was clad in a Chinese kimono and slippers.

The doctor went to her immediately, felt the pulse, and raised the eyelids. In a few seconds he had satisfied himself. He pursed his lips and turned to McLean.

"Dead!"

"How long?"

"Not more than an hour. But it doesn't seem like a police case to me. There is no sign of any wound."

McLean turned to the trembling maid.

"Was your mistress a healthy woman?"

"No, sir. She used to see the doctor pretty often, but I have only been with her a month."

"Why did you ring the police?"

"I—I didn't know what to do. I rang up the doctor first, but he was not at home. I—I thought if I telephoned the police they would send a doctor too."

"You left a message for the doctor?"

"Yes, sir. The maid said she expected him home at any minute."

"Are you the only other person in this house?"

"Yes, now. But the mistress has an Indian servant named Mehib Khan. Her husband was a Judge in India, and when he died the mistress brought Mehib with her. That was six years ago."

"Where is he now?"

"On holiday. He has a son studying in the University of Edinburgh—to be a doctor. I think the mistress was interested in the son. Mehib heard that his boy had just passed his first examination and asked permission to go to Edinburgh. He was to return the day after to-morrow. I thought the mistress would prefer me to stay in to-night as Mehib is away, but she said she did not mind my going out, and——"

She was cut short by a ring at the door. McLean told her to go and answer it, and a few seconds later an elderly man entered, carrying a small bag which betrayed his calling.

"I am Doctor Wilson," he said. "I understand you are from Scotland Yard?"

"Yes. I am Inspector McLean, and this is Doctor Gines. It rather looks as if we are not required."

"I think not. I have been attending Mrs. Laverton for some six years—valvular trouble. I anticipated some such ending, but not just yet. I'll take a look at her."

He carried out the usual examination, and was completely satisfied.

"She was a little headstrong," he mused. "Difficult to persuade her to take things easily." He turned to the maid. "What did your mistress do to-day?"

"She stayed at home all the morning, sir, but went to a theatre matinée this afternoon. I thought she looked very tired when she returned, sir."

"Hm! She might have lived for many years had she taken any care of herself."

"You are quite satisfied?" asked Gines.

"Perfectly. I am sorry you have been troubled. But the maid did what she thought was best."

Gines growled a little at having been dragged from a comfortable chair for nothing, but McLean did not complain. It was all part of life to him. He wondered who would get all Mrs. Laverton's charming furniture, and the wireless set reminded him that he had not yet invested in the latest plaything of science.

Things being unusually quiet he wandered into the Strand the next morning and looked over various sets. At last he was induced to pay quite a considerable sum for one of the newest type of sets, guaranteed to get Timbuctoo.

It was installed into McLean's flat on the following day, and he found yet another hobby to add to his full score. The next day he picked up the new issue of one of the well-known wireless journals, and was wondering whether it was really worth twopence, when his eyes fell on a letter from a correspondent:

"Sir,
"I was listening in at 9.30 on Tuesday night to 2LO, and distinctly heard conversa-

tion which could not possibly have come from the studio. It sounded like ' meb carne what are you doing—— ? ' I wonder if any others of your readers had a similar experience ?
"Yours faithfully,
"James Lightfoot."

Beneath was printed a note from the editor :

(Possibly a case of local induction caused by neighbouring telephone wire.)

McLean wrinkled his brows as his eyes fell on the appended address. It was 38 Cedar Avenue—a thoroughfare which ran at right angles to that in which Mrs. Laverton had lived. He paid the twopence and went home. An hour later he rang up Dr. Wilson.

"Inspector McLean speaking. When does the funeral of Mrs. Laverton take place ? "

"It took place this afternoon."

"Hm! Nuisance! That's all, thank you."

Early the following morning McLean was in Cedar Avenue. No. 38 was two houses from the corner—less than fifty yards from the house in which he had seen the dead woman. Stretched overhead were two wireless aerials in fairly close proximity to a telephone wire.

Mr. James Lightfoot was at home. McLean

gave his real name, but gave Lightfoot to understand that he was interested purely from a scientific point of view in the letter which he had read in the Radio Press. Would Mr. Lightfoot state exactly what he heard?

"Merely what I wrote. It was so clear it might have been next door. Yet I can't understand the words 'meb carne.' Of course it wasn't that—it couldn't be. Yet I could almost swear it was."

"A man's voice?"

"No—a woman's. Rather excited I thought."

"You heard nothing else?"

"Well, a noise that might have been anything—but no more speech."

McLean was a little surprised that the intelligent-looking Mr. Lightfoot did not suspect the telephone wire, nor connect the words "meb carne" with the native servant of Mrs. Laverton, but he concluded that Cedar Avenue was like most suburban places, where people lived all their lives without knowing many of their neighbours. Ultimately he thanked him and made his departure.

Subsequent inquiries elsewhere revealed the fact that Mehib Khan had benefited handsomely under the will of his late mistress, who referred to him as a faithful, loyal and loving servant. McLean cudgelled his brains to find a solution that would fit. Without sound grounds he could not hope for an exhumation order, and all he had to work upon at the moment were those words, presumably spoken just before the death of Mrs. Laverton: " Mehib Khan—what are you doing here ? " What could be plainer than the fact that Mehib Khan was not in Edinburgh on that night, but in London, and that he had called on his mistress ?

Even so, that in itself was no proof of murder or fell intent. A verdict of " Death from natural causes " had been given, nor could that verdict be rescinded until McLean could produce many more facts than he at present possessed. He blamed himself for not examining the room carefully on the occasion of his visit, but the doctor's emphatic report had disarmed him. To warn Mehib Khan by interrogating him was yet premature. The next link lay in Edinburgh. There a clever detective obtained proof positive that Mehib had never gone to visit his son. The boy stated that he had not seen his father for three months !

On receipt of this information McLean called on Mehib Khan. He found a tall, sleek Hindoo, garbed in European dress—a veritable idol of immobility. He invited McLean into the room where the death had occurred, and expressed his surprise at this call from the police.

" You believe your mistress died from heart failure ? " said McLean.

" That is so. For many years she suffer."

" You have known her for a long time ? "

"Twelve years—six in India and six here. When my master die I come with mistress to attend her. Mehib knew her desires. She love the Indian food, and Mehib cook it for her."

"She was very fond of you?"

"Yes, and very generous. She place my son in big university where he learn to be a doctor, and now she leave me this house and furniture—also money. It was more than Mehib expect—or deserve."

"She evidently thought otherwise. Now tell me where you were on the night she died."

"I go to see my son."

"When?"

"That same morning. The next day I see notice in the paper, and I come back—to find my poor mistress dead."

"You have known her have heart attacks?"

"Many—many times. The doctor he come often, and tell her she must rest quiet, but she take no notice and go out a lot. It is very sad, Sahib."

McLean agreed. The conversation was leading nowhere, but it afforded him an opportunity to endeavour to read what lay behind those dark velvet orbs, and he thought he detected just a trace of nervousness.

"It looks as if you cannot help me much," mused McLean.

"There is nothing to do. She die like so many —peacefully the doctor say. I do not understand why you come now——"

"I may be mistaken," said McLean. "I may be."

In the meantime he had taken in every detail of the room's contents. It was exactly the same as on his first visit, with one exception. The plant which had been in the porcelain bowl had gone, and in its place was another plant of quite a different species !

§

When McLean left the house he did not pass immediately into the avenue, but took a turn or two round the small garden. Once he turned abruptly and thought he saw a tall form move swiftly from the window of the sitting-room. It was obviously the Hindoo, and his nervous interest in McLean's investigations rather went to prove that his conscience was by no means as clear as it might have been.

What McLean was hunting for was discovered inside a very full dustbin. It was the plant which he had seen previously in the porcelain bowl. A transformation had taken place since then, for now its leaves were curled and dry, and its blossoms wilted. The earth which surrounded it was still there. The whole thing had been taken *en bloc* from the flower-pot inside the bowl and flung into the dustbin.

A few days before that plant had been the healthiest thing imaginable. Now it was dead! But the earth around it was moist. The cause of the plant's death was not at all evident, but McLean thought he knew it. An old newspaper was with the other rubbish. McLean shook the ashes from it and used it to wrap the plant in—earth and all. Then he concealed the parcel under his coat and made his way out.

That evening there was a conference at Scotland Yard. Three interested faces watched McLean as he took a paper from his pocket and read it aloud. It was a report from an analytical chemist, and it testified that the soil around the dead plant was impregnated with a chemical substance not yet identified—but a poisonous substance undoubtedly.

" What is your theory, McLean ? "

" Mrs. Laverton was poisoned, and the man who poisoned her used the flower-pot as a receptacle for the remains of the poison. He probably administered it in the glass which I saw by the side of the couch. Afterwards he washed out the glass—leaving it free of poison."

" You suspect the native servant ? "

" Who else ? He knew that the maid would be out. He probably had a key to the front door. He stood to benefit under the will of his mistress.

The fact that she suffered from valvular disease of the heart would render the job comparatively simple. I can prove that he never went to Edinburgh at all—that he lied to me when I questioned him."

"Your theory chiefly hangs upon that induction business?"

"To a great extent, but other facts bear that out. The doctor stated that he did not expect so sudden a collapse. I have seen him since and have read his medical memoranda. His patient was by no means in a bad state. No, sir—it was poison."

"Then what is the next step?"

"An exhumation order. I am convinced that an autopsy will reveal poison in the body. That will be a big step forward."

After some little delay the exhumation took place, while Mehib Khan was watched closely. The pathological expert gave a report which supported McLean's theory to the hilt. The poison—a very unusual one—proved to be the same as that found in the earth surrounding the plant. It was a triumph for McLean, but even yet the case bristled with difficulties.

"The induction business," said McLean's chief. "How do you account for that? We have but one man's statement that he heard a voice—purporting to be that of the dead woman, which if true would prove that the Hindoo entered that room at about nine-thirty, when he was supposed to be in Edinburgh. Can that phenomenon be explained?"

"I have technical opinion on the subject, sir. The thing has been known to happen before. A wireless aerial has been known to pick up messages from an adjacent telephone wire while a person is using that line."

"You suggest that the deceased was using the telephone when the murderer entered the room?"

"No. If chance induction was taking place, it would be an astonishing coincidence if the man who overheard, heard only what he alleged hearing. It is highly probable he would also have heard other conversation."

"But you agree that the telephone receiver must have been off the instrument in order to make the microphone sensitive?"

"Quite, but it might have been done by accident. The telephone was placed on a fairly high table near the door. Anyone entering might accidentally raise the receiver with his elbow—for just sufficient time for those few words to be overheard."

"Ingenious explanation! You think we should make an arrest?"

"I do, sir. It will be easier to search the house when Mehib Khan is in custody."

"You hope to find the bottle?"

"That would be conclusive."

"Well, go ahead."

That afternoon Mehib Khan was arrested on a charge of murder. He was indignant, and averred that he loved his mistress more than anyone in the world. Once he had saved her life, by sucking the venom of a snake from her ankle. He could prove that. It was unjust—a cruel and terrible aspersion!

With the house at his disposal, McLean instituted a thorough search. Not a single nook or cranny was left unexplored. A large number of small bottles was found, but none of these proved to be the one desired. Then when he was about to give up all hope McLean was successful. In the kitchen he found a loose board—underneath the linoleum. Upon lifting this a thin blue bottle was found between the joists. The label had been scraped off, and not a trace of it could be found. But McLean was more or less satisfied, and later the chemist identified the minute portion of liquid that remained in the bottle.

"A bad outlook for Mehib Khan," said the Assistant Commissioner. "He has just made a statement. Better read it."

McLean perused the typed and signed document. It was of considerable length, and gave the Hindoo's alleged movements from the time he left the house until the time he returned. On the night of the tragedy he swore he was in a certain hotel in Edin-

burgh, and that the manager, waiter and chambermaid would corroborate. McLean pursed his lips.
" That can't be true. But I will test it."
This was done through the Edinburgh police, and the result staggered McLean. Mehib's statement appeared to be true. As a Hindoo he was a conspicuous figure, and the servants as well as the manager recalled him easily. Still unconvinced, McLean called for an identification test. On the following day three witnesses identified Mehib Khan from a dozen very similar natives. The Assistant Commissioner looked down his nose. It was not often that McLean blundered.

It was then that a new possibility entered McLean's mind. It came like a ray of sunshine amid the gloom of intense disappointment.

" Give me two days, sir," he said. " There is a twist in this case, but I think I can see it. Hold Mehib."

§

That evening McLean travelled to Edinburgh with exhibit No. 1 in his pocket. It was a rather curious little bottle—so thin as to be unique. Knowing Edinburgh like his two hands, McLean recalled a certain chemist who issued bottles exactly similar. It was a coincidence that could not be overlooked—EDINBURGH.

Early the next morning he was at the chemist's,

taking with him both the bottle and the analyst's report. The man at the counter was rather a dunderhead, so McLean waited until the manager himself turned up.

" I'm a police officer," he said.

" Not the first to visit me. What's the trouble ? "

" Can you identify this bottle ? "

The manager nodded immediately he saw the thing.

" One of ours."

" You are positive ? "

" There is a means of proving it. All our poison bottles are marked with a small serial number on the bottom—practically invisible in ordinary light. We were involved in a bad murder case some years ago, and a member of the staff invented an easy means of identification. I'll see."

He took the bottle and disappeared into an inner office. Two minutes later he was back again.

" Ours," he said. " I have traced the serial number in the book."

" Did it contain that ? "

McLean pushed over the analyst's report, and the man inclined his head.

" To whom was it supplied ? "

" A medical student—a Hindoo named Ali Mehib Khan. Rather a rare prescription. He said he was experimenting on guinea-pigs."

" Date ? "

"June the eighteenth."

"You have the address of the student?"

"Oh, yes. It is in the book. I will make a copy for you."

McLean left the place in a state of suppressed excitement. The rest of the morning was spent in furtive inquiry, and it was established that on the night of the murder Ali was not in Edinburgh. His father had arrived there to find him missing. A call at the house where Ali lived revealed the fact that Ali was out, trying a new motor-car. McLean waited patiently at the end of the street. It was late in the evening when he saw a dapper little car appear at the other end of the street, and stop outside the house which he had visited. A lithe young man stepped out of the car and ran up the steps. McLean followed him. The door was shut by the time he reached it, but he rang and the maid came immediately.

"I want to see the gentleman who just came in," he said, and passed by her.

On the first floor Ali had his card attached to the door. McLean knocked and Ali appeared. He was a younger version of his father—keen-eyed, handsome and well-built.

"I am a police officer," said McLean, looking him straight in the eyes.

"C-come in!"

The room into which McLean stepped was clean

and tidy. There was a bookcase on the right filled with medical treatises, and a number of books on the table by the open window. Ali seemed to be calm enough, but McLean knew it was a clever piece of acting. He discerned all the slight nervous movements of a man who carries a great weight on his mind. Ali was waiting for him to speak, but he played upon the Hindoo's nerves by making observations about the furniture, books and the weather outside.

"What—what do you want—with me?" inquired Ali, now scarcely able to conceal his agitation.

McLean swung round on him fiercely.

"I have come to arrest you for the murder of Mrs. Laverton in London, on the evening of June 19."

"What!"

McLean produced the slim bottle from his pocket, and at the sight of it Ali lost his nerve. His eyes moved from side to side, and his lips opened slightly, without making the slightest sound.

"Come!" said McLean. "I must warn you that anything you may say——"

The next move was quite unexpected. Ali turned with the agility of a cat, sprang through the open casement window, and then jumped clean on to the pavement. Two seconds later he was in his car and moving away. McLean followed his example, and grunted as the hard pavement almost dislocated his joints. He ran after the swiftly moving car, and at the end of the street saw Ali about to turn a corner in the distance. Parked on the opposite side of the road was a big Daimler car. McLean ran towards it, jumped in and was away in a few seconds. Upon entering the house his keen eyes had taken in the number of Ali's car —a very necessary point, since it was growing dark. He turned where Ali had turned and saw a red light in the distance. His foot went down on the accelerator pedal and the Daimler shot forward.

Shortly afterwards he got a glimpse of the rear number-plate of the fugitive car. He had made no mistake—his quarry was there. Ali seemed to know the district well, for he avoided all main thoroughfares and made for the open country. The city was left behind and the race went on in the gathering darkness. McLean had forty horse-power under his bonnet, and yet the little car in front kept its distance.

Big risks were taken both by pursued and pursuer, and accidents avoided by hairs-breadths. McLean was now thoroughly warmed up. Once he found himself on Ali's tail, and could see the scared dark face as it turned slightly.

"Stop!" he roared.

But Ali had no intention of stopping, and his speedy car drew away once more. It was ten minutes later when disaster overtook him. With McLean hard upon him, he came upon the rear of a motor-bus travelling in the same direction. Either he had to slow down to fifteen miles an hour, or pass the big bus on a blind corner. He chose the latter alternative, and on the acute bend met a steam-waggon. There was a shrieking of brakes, a loud yell, then a horrid noise of crumpling steel and wood. . . . In the darkness Ali's battered body was extricated from the wreckage. The steam-waggon driver and McLean carried him to the Daimler.

Five miles on the road back to Edinburgh, McLean was obliged to stop, for it was evident that Ali was close to death. He was bleeding at the mouth and in great agony. McLean leaned over him.

"All—over!" muttered Ali. "I tell you—something. I—I kill the woman. She die—soon—any case. Father say he inherit much money when—she die. I owe much money—bookmaker—they worry me—threaten me. When I go to London house—months ago—I take mould of key—in wax. My father write last week—say he come see me. I pretend go away urgent mission—leave note for him. But I go London . . ."

He coughed and closed his eyes. McLean thought he was gone, but a little later he opened his eyes and spoke almost in a whisper.

"I—enter—house. Creep to room where she sit. As I enter door she see me and say something. I run at her—and the shock cause her heart to jump. She fall on—couch, faint a little, and then forget—ask for water. I give her—the poison in water—and—and——"

A choke and a groan, and he was gone. McLean pursed his lips and drove the body to Edinburgh.

Subsequently Mehib Khan was released. He bore the police no animosity, but the knowledge of his son's murderous act and base ingratitude left him a broken man. McLean saw him before he left. "There is just one point, Mr. Mehib Khan," he said. "You swore you had seen your son in Edinburgh. You must have known it was he who came to that house?"

"Yes. He leave behind him a handkerchief. I remember once he say to me it is a good thing when my mistress die. In Edinburgh I hear that he is in great debt. When the flower die—so strangely I suspect poison. Then I find the bottle —in the garden. I tear off the label and hide it— where you find it. I try to save my son. Allah will not punish me for that. Now let me go, for my spirit is sad. I would return to my native land."

McLean watched him depart, and reflected that but for his sudden interest in wireless no one would have dreamed that Mrs. Laverton died from anything but heart failure—save two men, who would have kept that secret for all time.

McLEAN INVESTIGATES VIII

§

IT was three months after the big Hatton Garden robbery, and Scotland Yard was still engaged in attempting to locate the "Emperor" diamond which was included in the booty taken by the thieves. It was one of the biggest stones in existence, and had but recently come from South Africa. The robbery had been carried out with great boldness and skill, and in addition to the enormous diamond some twenty thousand pounds' worth of other jewels had been taken.

The passing of one of the smaller stones had put the police on the right scent, and ultimately a gang of expert jewel thieves was run to earth in a night club near Soho. Resisting capture, the gang had put up a fight during which two detectives were injured and one of the gang killed, by jumping from a top-floor window into the street below.

Only one man was captured, and on his person were found a number of the less valuable stones. His record was a black one, and as a result he had been sent to Dartmoor for a term of five years. To all inquiries anent the "Emperor" diamond he kept a still tongue, but it was proved that he was hand in glove with the leading spirit of the gang—Murphy—now dead, and there seemed little doubt that he knew where the diamond was hidden.

"It may have gone out of the country?" mused the Assistant Commissioner.

McLean shook his head.

"I doubt it, sir. We got them too soon after the robbery. Murphy wouldn't have trusted a living soul with that stone. He meant to get away with it himself."

"But other booty was found on him."

"Yes. Stuff difficult to identify. The 'Emperor' was different. There wasn't a diamond merchant in the world who would not have recognised it. I am convinced that Murphy planted that stone earlier in the evening when he got news through someone that the police were after him. If we only knew where he was from seven p.m. until midnight it would help tremendously. But we don't. It was only by luck that Sergeant Brook saw him in Oxford Street five minutes after midnight. Shelley lost him in Piccadilly shortly before seven. He saw Shelley and gave him the slip."

"Hm. Have you any suggestions?"

"Yes. A rather bold one, but it may help. It involves very little risk. I propose we get into communication with the Governor of Princetown Jail and arrange to let Spragg escape."

"What!"

"If Spragg knows where the stone is hidden he won't stay away from it long. Give him a week or so of freedom and he'll lead us to the diamond —if, as we believe, he knows where it is."

"But the fellow is clever. He may get clean away!"

"No. That is where I come in. I propose to be put away for a stretch, with Spragg. It can be arranged that I work with his section—quite close to him. My idea will be to tempt him to escape on a suitable occasion. We shall—by arrangement —get clean away. After that I will keep in touch with headquarters—and Spragg. We can put him under lock and key at any time."

The Assistant Commissioner thought over the scheme. It was bold and irregular enough, but a hundred thousand pounds was involved, and the only alternative seemed to be to wait for nearly five years, until Spragg got his release in the ordinary way. He told McLean that it would be necessary to refer the matter to the highest quarters, and for two days McLean heard nothing. Ultimately he was called into a conference, and was told that his scheme would be tried without delay.

On the following day he went by train to the isolated prison in the heart of Dartmoor. There he was clad in convict garb and lodged in a cell. To all and sundry he was known as 535, and he

McLEAN INVESTIGATES

soon discovered that Spragg was 444. It was mid-winter and the weather was vile on the whole. But occasionally it was fine enough for his gang to work in the prison quarries, from which stone was being got to build two new warders' cottages. Very soon McLean was on speaking—or rather whispering—terms with Spragg. The latter was a man of middle age, who had suffered the loss of his left eye, and wore a black shade over it. His height was about the same as McLean's, and he was as hard as nails, having spent most of his adult years in prison.

"What's your stretch?" he asked McLean.

"Seven of the best—if I live as long in this rotten place."

"It's a picnic compared with Devil's Island. French place that would drive any fellow clean off his dot. Thank God I got out of there. Phew!"

"Been here long?"

"Three months. Careful—here's old Flap-Jack!"

The warder who suffered under this appellation came forward and reprimanded them for talking. McLean answered him back savagely and received a prod from the end of the rifle which the warder carried.

"God! I'd like to get him by myself—one dark night," growled Spragg. "No good cursing 'em, pard, when they hold all the cards. The time to do that is when you've got a length of lead pipe in your mitt. What did they get you for, anyway?"

McLean made a sign used among counterfeit coin men, and Spragg understood.

"Seven years is a good stretch for that," he mused.

"Yes. But a cop got hurt."

"Ah—I get you!"

It would have been madness to force matters, so McLean had to suffer all the discomforts of a real convict for many days ere he considered himself sufficiently friendly with Spragg to propose anything sensational. One day, in the quarry, he began to broach the subject. It was bitterly cold, with thick rime on the ground, and a good mist gathering. McLean shivered.

"I'm half frozen," he complained. "And sick to death with this rotten existence. What's to prevent a fellow from getting away?"

Spragg laughed grimly and nodded towards the warder's rifle.

"That," he said. "I've heard that only one man has ever succeeded in escaping from here. There's miles and miles of moorland, and they quickly put a ring of police round it."

"But if one man can do it, so can another."

"Lots have tried, and failed."

McLean got nearer to him.

"Can you keep a secret?"

"Guess I've kept a few."

"Well, when I knew the cops were after me I rented a little cottage not far from here, and another one near Broadmoor. It was odds on I'd be sent to one of those places if they ever got me. In the cottage are some clothes, money, and a motor-cycle. If I can reach that place I'll bet they never see me again. I know the moor like my two hands. There are a thousand ways of getting out of it without taking a single main road. I know a track, suitable for a motor-cycle, that avoids all roads for twenty miles. If this mist gets any thicker I'm going to have a shot at it."

Spragg thought deeply, and McLean saw that he was very agitated. Nothing more was said that day, but on the morrow Spragg mentioned the matter.

"Were you serious about what you said yesterday?"

"Yes, and this is the most promising time. Old Flap-Jack is getting nervous about the mist. I reckon he'll muster us and take us back in a few minutes."

"But there's the second warder."

"They dare not both leave the men. Look at the advantage I've got! When we leave the quarry and reach the place where the big rock projects, there is a sharp fall on the left. It leads to a stream, and that stream leads straight to the cottage—a matter of two miles. Why, a hundred men could get lost in this mist. I'm going to risk it. Why not take a chance with me?"

Spragg hesitated as he stole another glance at the armed warder.

"Maybe you aren't keen?"

"Keen! By G——!"

"Well, you'll never get another chance like this. I've a couple of suits in the cottage, and you can ride on the back of the motor-bike. We'll be in Exeter in two hours."

"You may be in hell."

McLean shrugged his shoulders. In any case he meant to make the attempt in the hope that Spragg would follow him at the last moment. Half an hour later his prognostication came true. The mist got so dense that the two warders decided it was dangerous to permit their desperate crowd to stay out of the prison any longer, and mustered them together. Spragg fell in, next to McLean.

"You're going to risk it?" he whispered.

McLean nodded.

"I'm with you."

"Good! Don't come with me. Break to the right and run down the slope until you reach the stream, then keep right along the bank. I'll pick you up——"

"Stop that talking, No. 535!" thundered a voice.

A few seconds later the group of convicts were

marching towards the prison. Spragg remembered the big projecting rock, and very soon it loomed through the mist. He turned his head slightly and received a quick glance from McLean. The head of the party reached the rock, and suddenly McLean dived away from the party. The watchful warder, having been warned of this escapade, fired to miss the vague leaping form. The second warder halted the men and came running up. As he passed Spragg the convict followed McLean's example, and disappeared into the mist.

Deep down in the dell the two escaped men found each other. Both were breathless, and Spragg's eyes were full of excitement. From above came the sound of a rifle and a muffled shout. McLean grinned and pointed ahead.

"That's the way. You keep immediately behind me. I'll take to the water further down in case they use dogs. I told you—this thing was as easy as falling off a log. The cottage is hidden in a wood. It will take them a month of Sundays to find it in this weather. Gosh, I'll be glad to get rid of these togs!"

§

After wading for a quarter of a mile in the stream, McLean and Spragg made the bank again, on the opposite side, and continued their journey. It was impossible to see more than a few yards ahead, but this did not trouble McLean, for he had previously placed a stake at the spot where it was necessary to turn off. He came upon the stake and drew it from the frozen ground.

"This is the place," he said. "There's a beaten track through the woods to the cottage. Only about three hundred yards."

It was now getting dark, and amid the thick timber it was difficult to see the ground. But ultimately they emerged into better light and a building loomed up before them.

"Is that it?" inquired Spragg.

"Yes. The door is locked, but the key is hidden in a cranny in the wall."

He searched along the broken-down wall, and produced a key. A few seconds later they were inside the cottage. It was poorly furnished and very damp. Illumination was supplied by a central paraffin lamp, and there was also an oil stove.

"Here are some matches," said McLean. "Get the stove going while I hunt up some clobber. We're in luck so far."

"Where's the bike?"

"In a shed at the back. I've some canned stuff in the cupboard and a bottle or two of beer. Rather smart me having this little place all ready for emergencies, eh?"

"Aye, you're smart you are."

McLean turned out a cupboard. It contained a

very good assortment of clothes, including boots and mackintoshes. From a desk he extracted about ten pounds in notes and cash, and then went in search of the beer. They changed before they regaled themselves.

"What are we going to do with that stuff?" inquired Spragg, pointing to their discarded garb.

"Sink it in the stream, with a lump of rock inside. I'll take it now."

He gathered up the boots as well, but it was then that Spragg remembered something. He took his left boot, and slipped his hand inside. The sock-lining came loose and a folded piece of paper came to view.

"Money?" inquired McLean.

"No. Maybe I'll tell you later."

McLean nodded casually, and took away the pile of discarded things. He disposed of them and came back to find Spragg already drinking.

"Good stuff! There's yours. Is the bike all ready?"

"Yes—with a full tank. There isn't a sound outside."

"Can you ride the bike in this mist?"

"Easily. I've got a powerful acetylene lamp on the forks. It can be dipped."

"Well, let us be getting. I shan't feel safe until we are out of the moor."

They finished up their beer and McLean went

for the motor-cycle. He wheeled it round to the front of the cottage, lighted the head-lamp and pushed down on the self-starter. It refused at first, but a second attempt set the engine going.

"Hell of a noise!" grumbled Spragg.

Once through the gate Spragg mounted the carrier, and McLean started away along a rough and narrow track. The powerful acetylene lamp enabled him to see about twenty yards ahead, so progress was reasonably rapid. Now and again the track degenerated into open moorland and scattered rocks, and the passenger was treated to the most severe bumping.

For half an hour things went fairly well, and then McLean realised that he had lost his way. Peering through the mist he drove at a slower rate, for there were innumerable pitfalls and obstacles. Spragg made some remark to him, and he was about to reply when the back tyre burst with a terrific report, and the machine swung sideways and brought the driver to the ground. He scrambled to his feet and, to his amazement, found his passenger gone.

"Spragg!" he called.

A queer echo came back to him. He raised the fallen machine and the bright light struck in a new direction. He gasped to see the edge of a quarry within two yards of him. The frost on the grass close to it was disturbed. He knelt down and called. From below came a deep groan.

McLean stood up and groped his way round the quarry. At last he found a descending path and went down it. By the length of it the quarry was of enormous depth, and if the drop had been vertical, then Spragg was doomed. A small pocket torch which he had brought from the cottage helped him to locate the convict. He was lying on his back with one knee up in a curious manner. The light fell on a contorted face.

" Spragg ! "

" I—I'm done."

It was obvious he was speaking the truth. Death was only a matter of minutes.

" Do you—good turn," he muttered. " Inside pocket—paper——"

McLean found the paper referred to. It was a plan of certain London streets, with a red line marking several of them. But where the plan had been folded was a tear. The bottom part was missing.

" You'll have to go—Hymen—Hymen, Duke Street, Pimlico. He—he got—other half. Plan of a hotel—where a big diamond is hid. Murphy hid it. When he jumped—killed himself—Hymen and I found him. Wasn't quite dead then. Asked us to post a letter—addressed to his sister. We guessed he was letting her in on—diamond. I opened the letter—just as police arrived. But Hymen snatched at it and got the bottom half before I could find the name of the hotel. Go to Hymen—do a deal with him. He knows where the stone is hid, but not the hotel. You can find that—by the plan. But take care—cunning swine——!"

He died a few minutes later. McLean took a pistol from his pocket and fired it several times at intervals. Half an hour passed, and then he heard voices from above. Evidently someone had found the motor-cycle.

"Hullo!" he shouted.

A reply came back, and a few minutes later three men armed with rifles appeared through the mist—warders from the prison. McLean recognised one of them as "Flap-Jack."

"An accident," he said. "The thing didn't go exactly to plan. But I have what I wanted. Have you got a car?"

"Yes—half a mile back—on the road."

"Then I'll come with you. I want to get to London to-night if possible."

The dead body of Spragg was taken back to the prison, and an hour later McLean left for London. The mist was quite local, and the express train landed him in London before midnight. He regretted the accident, but was grateful for what he had learnt. The next step was to find Mr. Hymen.

§

A week later Paul Hymen sat in his flat in Pimlico with three confederates. Two of these were men and the other was a woman. Hymen produced a half-sheet of paper from his pocket and gazed at it for the thousandth time. It bore the plan of a big building, and in a certain spot a red cross was marked.

"A hotel," he mused. "But where? We must have been in five hundred hotels, and never a sign of the darn thing. Enough to drive a fellow mad."

"Can Spragg have got it?"

"I don't think so. I just got a glimpse of his half of the paper before the police set us running. It was a plan of streets. He might know the street —even the hotel, but not the actual spot. It would be like looking for a needle in a haystack."

"But he escaped—a week ago. I'll bet he came out to lay his hand on the ' Emperor.' "

"He may come to me yet."

"But a week!"

"Fool! He would have to lie pretty close with all the police after him. I don't believe he has got the diamond. I knew Murphy. He would plant it cunningly. Gosh, if we could only land it!"

They sat on for some time, drinking and playing cards, but their interests were not there. In all their eyes was written greed. Each one of them saw that gorgeous stone, waiting for an owner, and weeks and weeks of searching had only added to their natural avarice. It was close upon ten o'clock when there came a knock on the door, and Hymen went to open it himself. He saw on the threshold a man with one eye and a black eye-shade —a face bearing six days' growth of beard—lean jaws and a dirty neckerchief.

" Spragg ! " he gasped.

" Aye. I thought you didn't recognise me."

" Well, you look different."

" So would you if you had suffered hell for three months and been without food for a week. Let me in for God's sake ! I saw a cop looking at me just now."

Hymen's eyes gleamed. What he had hoped for had come true. He conducted his welcome visitor into the sitting-room. The three occupants stared.

" Is it—Spragg ? "

" Give him a drink. He's nearly dead."

The visitor drank the glass of whisky at one gulp and then sat down. He looked at Hymen, and winked his single eye.

" Guess you know why I've come, eh ? "

" I've a good idea. The ' Emperor,' eh ? "

" Yes."

" You've got—the paper ? "

"Yes, but it's no good by itself. I want to know how we stand in the matter?"

"What do you suggest?"

"I want half."

Hymen frowned.

"What about Kate, and Tim and Harry? They've wasted weeks hunting——"

"That's not my fault. I didn't want them to hunt. Anyway, you can settle up with them. You'll have plenty to spare. With me it's fifty-fifty or nothing."

"Not so fast," put in Kate. "Suppose Paul ain't doing any business on those terms, what do you get then? Nix. It isn't for you to dictate."

The visitor stood up.

"Them's my terms," he said stubbornly. "If you don't like 'em I'll get out. Maybe I'll find the thing without——"

"Wait!" interrupted Hymen. "You shut your mouth, Kate. No need to go off the deep end, Spragg. I'll agree on your terms. Where's the paper?"

"In another place. You didn't think I was fool enough to bring it here, did you?"

"Why not?" snarled Hymen. "I play straight, don't I?"

"Well, anyway, I know the street and the place, but we can't go there to-night. Too many people. I'll meet you to-morrow morning outside here, at ten o'clock. Don't keep me hanging about. There's a police beat up the next street, and this damned eye of mine is awkward—for me. It's a deal, eh?"

"Sure! Have another drink?"

"No. I want all my wits. Just look through the window. I didn't like the look of that cop."

He gave a haunted look towards the window, and Hymen peered through it into the street below.

"Can't see anyone," he said. "You'll be all right. To-morrow morning—ten o'clock."

The visitor was shown out, and Hymen came back rubbing his hands.

"I knew he'd come. The fool can't find the 'Emperor' without me."

"Why the hell should he have half?" blurted Kate. "There are four of us, and only one of him."

Hymen took another drink and winked his eye.

"Do you think I'm mad enough to give him half? Now listen! I want you three to stay here to-morrow morning. When I've got the diamond I'll bring Spragg back here in a taxi. We've got him by the short hairs. All we have to do is to fix him up safe in the coal-cellar and take the first boat to the Continent. When we get there, a telephone message will bring the police down on him—and back he goes to quod."

His confederates were all agreeable. Spragg was

a comparative stranger to them, and they had only come in touch with him through the dead man—Murphy. In any case they had no scruples when playing for big stakes.

On the morrow Spragg turned up to time. Hymen saw him from the window, and immediately went down to him. The pair hurried away and soon found a taxi. Spragg told the driver to drop them at a particular spot in South Kensington.

"All that way out," mused Hymen. "No wonder we couldn't find the place. What's the name of the 'pub'?"

Spragg hesitated and then produced the piece of paper. Hymen ran his keen eye over the streets until he came to the spot where the red line ended.

"Didn't know there was a hotel there."

"There is—a new one. The 'Arcadia.' Quite a swell place."

"I believe you're right."

"Right! Why I've been——"

Hymen grinned.

"So you did have a shot at finding it?"

"Yes. But I didn't know where to look. Say, you're going to play straight over this?"

"Of course I am. We'll go straight back to the flat and then get a few things together and get across the Channel. Ah—here we are!"

The taxi stopped and they alighted. After a few

L

minutes' walk they reached the hotel. It was quite an imposing building, and boasted a winter garden that was open to non-residents. As soon as Hymen entered the vestibule he knew he was in the right place. The lay-out agreed exactly with the plan in his possession.

"You're right," he said. "Come right through —into the winter garden. We'll order drinks there."

They passed through the vestibule into the winter garden. At that early hour it was deserted, and Hymen suddenly remembered that intoxicating drinks could not be got. There were palms down both sides. He counted those on the left—one, two, three, four—and then chose the table nearest the fourth. The waiter came at once.

"No chance of a whisky?"

"Sorry, sir."

"Well, two lemonades."

The waiter left and Spragg looked at Hymen eagerly.

"Where is it?"

"You'll see—in a moment. Let us get rid of that damned waiter first."

The lemonades were brought, and the two men made an effort to talk casually. Then the waiter left, and Hymen's keen eyes followed him to the exit. Immediately the door closed he went to the big palm, and started to prod the earth around it.

Two minutes passed and nothing emerged from the disturbed soil.

"Watch that door, Spragg!"

"I'm watching."

More furious digging, and then a low exclamation. Spragg made a curious gesture towards the entrance, just before Hymen came to him with bulging eyes, and a great diamond enclosed in his right hand.

"Let's get—let's get——!" he gurgled, and then his face tightened up as he saw a neat little automatic pointed at him.

"Sit down there!" said the calm voice of McLean.

"What the devil——! Are you mad?"

McLean removed the black shade from his eye and blinked at the unaccustomed light. Hymen's face went pallid.

"My God! You're—a cop!"

Despite the pistol he turned to run, but found two stalwart men in plain clothes barring the way.

"Ah, Brook," said McLean. "You might attend to our friend. And I think that little sparkler will be safer in my care. Thanks! What a blessing binocular vision is! I hope I'll never see an eye-shade again. I'll see you later. I think a shave is very clearly indicated."

An hour later McLean was as immaculate as usual, but his chin smarted, and he prayed that his next case would not call for such personal sacrifices.

McLEAN INVESTIGATES IX

§

McLEAN sat in the consulting-room of his friend Dr. John Brealy, sampling one of the latter's very choice Havanna cigars. He had made the acquaintance of Brealy some years back in connection with a curious case, and had met him at intervals ever since. Brealy had made great progress since those days, and was now domiciled in a very fine house in Wimpole Street, and looked upon by the whole of his profession as a man with a great future.

"It was good of you to come, McLean," he said. "I was going to call on you, but have had a strenuous day, and am dog-tired."

"I wish I could make the same complaint," replied McLean. "With us things are exceptionally quiet. The world seems to be improving. If it goes on like this I shall soon be reduced to holding up motorists for exceeding the speed limit. But what is your trouble?"

"A little anxiety concerning a patient of mine. He is a wealthy Indian merchant—retired, and I have been attending him for about two months."

"An Indian?"

"Oh no—English. But he has spent most of his life in India. The case was a comparatively simple one. Valvular trouble, which was aggravated by too much liquid refreshment. I put him on the water-waggon and prescribed complete rest. He should have got better, but he doesn't. He gets worse."

" Is that extraordinary ? "

" Yes—in the circumstances. He is now confined to his room, and I am able to state positively that he gets no alcohol of any kind. His real trouble is disappearing, but there are strange complications. In fact I suspect poison."

" Ah ! "

" The symptoms point to that, and I am ready to stake my professional reputation on that theory."

" You have no idea how he gets it ? "

" None at all. So far as I can gather, all the members of his household are trustworthy. Certainly the cook is a native, but his niece assures me that the fellow is devoted to his master, and was cook to him in Bombay for over twenty years."

" Why bring a cook from India ? "

" A fad. Lawton—that is his name—Lawton got used to Indian diet. You must remember that practically all his life was spent in India. Habits are not given up easily."

" Who else is in the house ? "

" Two maids, and a butler named Stamp. The only other person is Miss Longdon—the niece. A charming woman of about thirty. And I should mention a night-nurse, engaged at my suggestion. Miss Longdon is also a qualified nurse, and looks after her uncle during the day."

" Lawton is wealthy, you say ? "

" Undoubtedly. A man worth nearly half a million."

" Is he aware of what is happening ? "

" No. I have, of course, kept my suspicion entirely to myself. I am telling you now because my patient is on the decline, and I am completely baffled."

" The patient has medicine ? "

" Yes, but it is always administered by the nurse."

" In fact you suspect no one ? "

" I have no reason to. But the fact remains he is getting poison into his system."

" Can I come along on your next visit ? You can introduce me as an interested confrère ? "

Brealy was agreeable, and on the following day McLean altered his normal appearance and accompanied the doctor to a big house at Hendon. The place was handsomely furnished, and had rather an Eastern touch about it, for Lawton had brought home with him many wonderful carpets and ornaments. The butler opened the door, and McLean scanned him keenly. He was about middle age, and refined. McLean felt inclined to rule him out at once. In the hall they met Miss Longdon—a tall, beautiful woman with soft, wistful eyes and a marvellous mass of auburn hair.

"I am so glad you have come, doctor," she said, and then halted as she saw McLean.

"Er—Doctor McLean," said Brealy, introducing his companion. "He is interested in your uncle's case."

"I fear he is worse this morning," she said. "I have just tried to get you on the telephone."

"Nurse Gibson is off duty?"

"Yes. She went to her room an hour ago, but told me to wake her if you asked for her."

"I don't think it will be necessary, but I will let you know. Come, McLean!"

The two men entered the sick-room, and found the patient looking extremely weak. Brealy examined him while McLean endeavoured to wear a professional air. It was obvious that Brealy was worried, for his examination was lengthy and minute. On the left of the bed was a table with a cupboard beneath, and on opening the door of the latter McLean saw some bottles and other paraphernalia. On the right was a massive wardrobe in walnut. There were two communicating doors —one leading to a bathroom and the other to a bedroom. Upon inquiring, McLean was told that Miss Longdon occupied the adjoining room.

She had gone out for a few minutes, but returned while Brealy was terminating his examination. Her eyes were full of sympathy and anxiety, and when she caught her uncle's eye she forced a smile of reassurance. There was little doubt in McLean's mind that she was genuinely concerned about his welfare.

"He must be kept very quiet," said Brealy. "Would you like me to send you up a day-nurse?"

"Oh no. I want to look after him. I am sure he would prefer that."

The patient nodded to endorse this statement, and Brealy did not force the point. He gave Miss Longdon a few instructions and promised to call the next morning. As soon as they left the house he became very grave.

"Bad—very bad!"

"He gets weaker?"

"Yes. There is devilish work going on here. What steps do you suggest, McLean?"

"I want to get into the house. Occasional visits are useless. The butler might be taken into your confidence. He can go sick and a temporary man can be engaged. You can recommend me."

"But Miss Longdon will recognise you?"

"I think not. A little hair-dye, the removal of this patch of bristles on my lip, a change of garb—and it is surprising what results can be effected. Even if she did recognise me, it would not be a disaster. We might confide in her, but I should prefer to keep my business a complete secret if that can be achieved."

"But that means eliminating the butler as a possible culprit?"

"Yes. But results will prove, or disprove, his innocence. If Lawton suddenly improves I will admit that my faith in the butler's integrity is ill-founded. We shall see."

Brealy promised to endeavour to bring about the change of staff, and was successful after the lapse of four days. The butler was confined to his room, with an imaginary illness which Brealy averred would keep him there for some weeks, and steps were taken to find a temporary man. Miss Longdon, with her hands very full, accepted Brealy's offer to settle this little problem for her, and Brealy sent up McLean for her approval.

Since Brealy himself had failed to recognise McLean in his new "make-up," it was scarcely likely that a woman who had only seen him for a few minutes would do so. He looked the perfect butler—a sleek, scrupulously clean individual, with black hair plastered well back over his forehead, a deferential but not obsequious air, and a noble deportment. Miss Longdon approved of him instantly and engaged him on the spot.

§

McLean's subsequent experiences, if not thrilling, were certainly enlivening. The parlourmaid—

Elsie, a girl of very romantic temperament—fell for him instantly. To her he was at once the Admirable Crichton, Beau Brummel and Rudolph Valentino rolled into one. The housemaid—Annie, while admitting "Mr. Tyler's" attractiveness—considered him cold and unfeeling.

"Hasn't got a 'eart," she complained. "Blooming mystery I call 'im."

That was just the attractive part of it to Elsie. She loved mystery men, and in her case "Mr. Tyler" unbent at intervals, and permitted her to gossip about the "master" and Miss Longdon.

"If Mr. Lawton should die," she said, "all his money will go to Miss Longdon. Isn't she lucky?"

"But how do you know?"

"Well, he's got no other relatives, and is very fond of her. He hasn't even made a will."

"My dear girl, how on earth can you possibly know——?"

"But I do! It was only a little while ago—just after he started his illness—that his solicitor came to see him. I heard the solicitor tell him it was his duty to make a will. But he just laughed, and then said that was like signing his death-warrant."

"I once knew a girl who caught a shocking cold putting her ears to keyholes," observed McLean.

Elsie looked guilty and then hurt. The conversation did not help McLean greatly. It was fairly obvious that will or no will Miss Longdon would benefit considerably from her uncle's death. But he could not bring himself to believe that there was guile in that alluring woman.

The cook, was an unknown quantity. He was a marvel of proficiency, and a glutton for work. In addition to possessing a knowledge of Indian diet, he was skilled in French cookery, and also the more solid British—which he held in contempt. He regarded himself as the servant of his sick master, and of nobody else. Miss Longdon had warned McLean that he was best left alone. But McLean had no intention of leaving him alone. He had it from Brealy that the poison was still being administered to the patient, and food was the first thing to come under suspicion.

Secretly he took samples of the very sparse meals supplied to the patient, but upon analysis everything was found to be perfectly wholesome. He turned his attention to the medicine, and this brought both Miss Longdon and the night-nurse under suspicion, since the medicine was administered by one or the other in turn, and one afternoon he made a startling discovery. A new bottle of medicine had been sent up, and he heard Miss Longdon rating the maid for having omitted to replace the used medicine glass with a clean one. The girl brought a fresh glass, and a few minutes later Miss Longdon left the sick-room. She told

McLean that her uncle was sleeping and that she was obliged to go out for a few minutes.

As soon as she had left McLean went into the sick-room. The patient was lying quite still, with his eyes closed, and on the table beside him was an empty glass and a medicine bottle. He noticed that the bottle was minus one dose, but to his disappointment the glass was perfectly clean. Evidently she had washed it out after using it. He opened the cupboard underneath the table, and was examining one of two bottles when he came upon another glass. It was dirty, and he came to the conclusion that the careless maid had put it back there instead of taking it downstairs. He took it away with him, and later that evening had the small contents analysed. The result bore out all Brealy's suspicions. It contained quite a fair proportion of arsenic. He went straight from the chemist to Brealy.

" You are not giving Lawton any arsenic in his medicine, doctor ? "

" No. Why do you ask ? "

" It's there."

" What ! "

" Here is an analyst's report on some dregs which I found in a medicine glass."

Brealy took the sheet of paper and perused the report. He looked very grim as he raised his eyes to McLean.

"So that's it?"

"It would account for his symptoms?"

"Yes. But who gives it to him?"

"That is what I have to find out. The night-nurse is absolutely above suspicion—of course?"

"She must be. What interest could she possibly have in poisoning her patient? Besides, I have known her for years. No—you must rule that out."

"Then it leaves—Miss Longdon."

"But she is devoted to her uncle, and would give her life for him. No, there is some other solution. Someone must gain access to that room."

"But would the patient take medicine from anyone but his nurses?"

"He might—in moments of semi-unconsciousness."

McLean pursed his lips, for the case was becoming extremely interesting. He had had time to examine the patient's charming niece, and like Brealy he was convinced of her devotion to her uncle. Yet there were one or two curious points in her behaviour. On two occasions he had seen her looking very strange—almost ill. On one occasion he had asked her—deferentially as befitted his position—if she were unwell, and she had passed by him as if she had not heard him. At nights, too, when she was relieved by the nurse, she would make a hasty meal and go out, returning very late.

Also she appeared to receive an unusually large

number of telephone calls, and sometimes she would disappear for half an hour or so, after receiving one of these. It was always a man who called—and he would give no name. These facts puzzled McLean, and he began to wonder whether his trust in the girl was fully justified.

On the next occasion when she went out, McLean entered her bedroom and carried out a detailed examination. At the back of the right-hand drawer in her dressing-table was a small bottle. He withdrew the cork, and one look at the contents was enough. It was arsenic!

The discovery startled him. Her acting had been consummate all through. He had seen her in tears when Brealy made it clear to her that her uncle was at a dangerous pass—while all the time she was undoubtedly giving him poison. And with what other object than that she should inherit his considerable wealth?

He stole into the adjoining room, and found an empty bottle into which he poured the poisonous liquid. Then he washed out the arsenic bottle and refilled it with plain water, which he subsequently coloured green. He had scarcely done this when Miss Longdon returned. He was in the sick-room at the moment, and was ready with a plausible excuse. But she did not question him. She went straight to her own room, and he heard a drawer being opened. Instead of retiring he concealed himself round the end of the massive wardrobe and waited.

She entered the room, now attired in a different dress, and an apron. The patient stirred and she gazed at him in a curious way. Then she went to the little table and found the medicine and glass. A dose was poured out, and while McLean observed her she slipped her hand into the pocket of her apron and produced the small bottle whose dangerous contents he had just changed. Two drops were introduced into the medicine, and the bottle replaced in her pocket. Approaching the bed she raised the patient carefully in her arms and administered the dose. He opened his eyes.

" Ah—Stella ! Medicine again—ugh ! "

She made no response, and the patient said no more, for the physical effort tired him. McLean watched her go back into her own room. Again there was the noise of an opening drawer. The thing was done—before his very eyes. It was incredible !

Brealy came that evening, and found his patient no worse. He took an opportunity to have a few words with McLean.

" Any further progress ? "

" Yes."

" In what direction ? "

" Your patient ought to begin to improve from to-day."

"You have found the source of the poison ? "

" Yes."

" Who administered it ? "

" I would rather defer answering. There are one or two points that are not quite clear. But in a day or two I hope to have everything unravelled."

On the following day McLean again managed to observe the administering of the medicine, by concealing himself in the wardrobe, and peering through the keyhole. But on this occasion there was no appearance of the arsenic bottle. It gave him furiously to think.

§

Two days later the telephone bell rang, and he answered it. A man's voice inquired for Miss Longdon—the voice he had heard many times. He went to her and she came to the instrument. A few minutes later she came to tell him that she had to go out for a little while, and begged him to take an occasional look at her uncle. He bowed, but had no intention of staying in the house. From the library window he saw her leave the place and make down the main drive, but instead of leaving the grounds she took a side path that cut through a shrubbery. McLean immediately went through the French window and followed her. The big garden was well wooded and there was ample cover for him. On the north side was an ivy-clad wall, and projecting above the wall were the head and shoulders of a man. McLean was obliged to halt behind a big tree, and from there he saw Miss Longdon greet her secret lover. He clambered over the wall, embraced her closely and then walked with her to a large summer-house in a secluded corner of the grounds. There was no means of overhearing what went on inside without taking the risk of being seen, so McLean waited until the girl emerged.

About twenty minutes passed and then she came out, with her lover holding her arm. He said something and pointed to the house. She nodded in a dazed way, and then left him. McLean at once ran towards the house and entered it first. He went straight to Miss Longdon's room, and found the arsenic bottle. Quickly he poured the innocent contents into a flower-pot and replaced the bottle. Then he concealed himself round the end of the wardrobe in the sick-room.

A few minutes passed and she came in, and went to her room as before. She came back, poured out the medicine and produced the small bottle. But when she tipped it nothing came out. That seemed to bewilder her for a second or two, but ultimately she administered the medicine and went back again to conceal the small bottle. McLean went outside and knocked on the door. Some minutes passed before she responded to the summons, and then she gazed at him blankly as if she did not recognise him.

" I did not know you were back, Miss," he said. " You told me to keep an eye on the master ? "

" The master ! Oh yes—yes. Of course, Tyler —of course. It's all right. I—I forgot."

He went away, and a little later entered the summer-house in the garden. It was quite a big building and comprised two rooms, one of which was given up to certain gardening tools. This room was at the rear of the main room, and was locked, but he managed to find the key of it. Two minutes later he telephoned to Brealy. Brealy met him by appointment in the garden.

" Well ? "

" The trap is laid. It may succeed. I hope it will, but I shall need you as a witness. To-morrow afternoon Miss Longdon may receive a telephone message. It usually comes about three o'clock. I want you to be here, just behind the summer-house, from two-thirty—in case that call comes. Keep well hid, and I will join you as soon as I can. Is that convenient ? "

" I will make it so if it will help my patient."

" Your patient is no longer in any danger. But I want to lay my hands on a certain person."

The thing was agreed upon, but two days passed before McLean was able to carry out his plan. The telephone bell rang, and he was at hand to answer it. Miss Longdon was inquired for, and he at once went to her. While she was on her way downstairs McLean left the house and joined Brealy. They at once entered the room of the summer-house—Brealy in a state of complete mystification. McLean begged for complete silence and pointed to two holes which he had bored in the partition—and which were now plugged with rag. Five minutes later the sound of approaching voices was heard. Two persons subsequently entered the adjoining room and sat down. McLean carefully removed the plugs—using one peep-hole himself, and leaving the other for Brealy.

Sitting with their backs to them were Miss Longdon and a man with dark hair. His arm was round her shoulder and he was talking in a tense and penetrating voice.

" How is your uncle, darling ? "

" Just the same. He seems to make such poor progress. I am very worried."

" You have told him nothing—about us ? "

" Oh no. He is too ill to discuss such a thing. When he is better I will tell him. But I am afraid it will mean parting from him—losing his friendship for ever. He hates you ever since that law case."

" Well, he got the best of it," he said bitterly. " Stella, darling, we must get married soon. His consent does not matter. You are a woman, and our happiness is at stake. You do love me, dear ? "

"Yes—yes. More than life. But it is wrong for me to leave him in the afternoons, when I should be nursing him. But when you ask me to come to you—somehow I can't help myself. But I can't stay a moment——"

"Wait—wait! Look at me, dear—look straight into my eyes. I want to know—to feel that you love me above everything else. Look at me!"

McLean touched Brealy on the arm, and the doctor saw the dark face come round slightly. The man's hands were on her shoulders and he was staring with tremendous intensity into her eyes. Then one hand left her shoulder and made a queer kind of pass. The doctor's breath came in gasps. He saw there the professional hypnotist. The woman's will was going.

"You remembered what I told you?"

"Yes—yes."

"You used the stuff in the bottle—two drops?"

"No. It was empty—all gone."

The voice was dull—lifeless.

"All gone! And he is alive still! Strange. But you must wait here. Don't move. Stay just like that for a few minutes. I shall not be long."

A pass or two and he rose and left the summer-house hastily. The girl sat there, perfectly motionless. Three or four minutes passed and he returned.

Again he faced her and took a small bottle from his pocket.

"Take this. Use it as before. Two drops in the medicine and then take the bottle and hide it at the back of the drawer. You will go now and do this—at once."

"Yes—yes."

Brealy gasped, and McLean touched his arm. In two seconds both men were on the other side of the partition, and McLean was facing the man, who was pressing the bottle into his victim's hands.

"With your permission I will take that bottle," said McLean.

The dark face became contorted with rage.

"How dare——? Who the devil are you?"

"Inspector McLean of Scotland Yard," snapped McLean. "And I am going to arrest you on a charge of conspiring to murder. Put out your hands!"

Less than an hour later the man was under lock and key.

McLean came back to the house to find Brealy there still. He was glad to inform the detective that his patient was now making a turn for the better.

"And Miss Longdon—does she know what part she played?"

"Not yet. I had great trouble in bringing her round. I fear that devil has undermined her health by the regular use of his power over her. Who is he?"

"His name is Da Silva, and he is Spanish. He took the house next door some three years ago, but had a quarrel with Lawton over their respective boundaries. Lawton started an action and won it. Since then they have been deadly enemies. It was because of that that Stella Longdon dared not tell him she was in love with their neighbour. Da Silva's motive was not so much hate as gain. Once Lawton was dead he could marry a very desirable heiress."

"Poor deluded girl! And we've got to disillusion her."

"Yes, but not yet," replied McLean. "I propose you get Lawton away from England to speed up his recovery. She will, of course, go with him. Mr. Da Silva's sudden disappearance will puzzle her, but the truth—which must come—will be less crushing when she has benefited by a removal from his sphere of influence. In the meantime you might inform her that her temporary butler has taken French leave. I assure you there will be wailing and gnashing of teeth in the servants' hall. Poor Elsie!"

McLEAN INVESTIGATES X

§

IT was nearly eleven o'clock on a bitter December night when McLean arrived at the house in Regent's Park, accompanied by the police doctor. He had been rung up to be informed that a suicide had taken place, and owing to a temporary shortage of staff, due to a bad epidemic of influenza, he had taken on the job himself.

They were let in by a pallid maidservant, who still wore her coat and hat, lending the impression that she had recently returned from an evening out. McLean asked her what had happened, and, almost speechless, she led him to the kitchen door, which was locked. A strong smell of gas assailed his nostrils and he bade the girl open all the windows and doors. When she came back he was trying to force an entry into the kitchen.

"You told me it was suicide," he said.

"It must be. I went into the garden and looked through the window. With the aid of an electric torch I was able to see the mistress. Her—her head is inside the gas oven. The window was latched and there was paper wedged between the sashes. There is some under this door too."

McLean had already observed that fact. He sent the girl to turn off the gas at the meter, and then proceeded to prise open the door with the blade of a small hatchet. Ultimately the lock gave and a great volume of gas belched out. McLean held his breath and went to the window, which he unlatched and opened at the top. The doctor immediately switched on the light and gave all his attention to the woman.

She was young—not more than twenty, and her head was resting on a large red cushion in the lower part of the gas-oven. It needed but one look at her to see that she was beyond human aid. In life she had been beautiful, but now——

"Too late?" queried McLean.

"Yes. Dead an hour I should say."

McLean sent the maid away while he examined the place. On the table was an inkpot and a pen. Under the inkpot was a half-sheet of white paper, with a message written on it, in neat and very firm handwriting.

> "I cannot bear the pain any longer. My head is terrible to-night. At times I feel that my reason is going. I have tried to be patient, but it is no use. Better the soft arms of death than this continual misery. I should like all my personal belongings to be sent to my sister. Please forgive me. . . ."

"Poor girl!" mused the doctor. "But is she the only occupant of this place?"

"We will find out—later. Don't step on that piece of paper. I want to examine it."

He picked up the folded sheet of newspaper which had been used to close up the chink under the door, and examined it with such minuteness that the doctor was puzzled.

"It's a clear case, isn't it?" he inquired.

"It may be."

"But look at the circumstances—the plugged door and window. Her letter——"

McLean was not listening. He took the key from the lock, looked at it and put it into his pocket. Then again he turned his attention to the note. Picking up the pen he dipped it in the ink and wrote a word or two on the back of the note.

"Interesting," he mused, as he surveyed his handiwork.

"Why?"

"The note was never written with this pen."

"It might have been written in another room and brought in here. Probably that pen was on the table, and has no connection with the note. A coincidence."

"That is possible. I will now question the maid."

He found the girl in the sitting-room—quite distracted, and in order to spare her feelings he interrogated her there.

"What was the dead woman's name?" he inquired.

"Russell—Miss Phyllis Russell."

"Age?"

"Twenty, I think."

"Did she live here alone?"

"Oh no. Mr. Russell—her uncle—lives here usually. But he had to go to Paris three days ago."

"Is he in business?"

"No. But he does writing sometimes—articles for the newspapers and stories. A very clever gentleman."

"You have his address?"

"Yes. He sent a card on his arrival in Paris."

"When does he return?"

"To-morrow, or the next day."

"When did you last see your mistress alive?"

"At ten o'clock this morning. My brother was married to-day and I had asked for the day off. I returned at half-past ten this evening, and to my surprise found the key in the front door. I thought Miss Russell had gone to bed, and did not want to be disturbed. But as soon as I entered I smelt the gas. I tried to get into the kitchen, and when I found the door locked I found an electric torch and went into the garden."

"Did you expect anything like this to happen?"

"Oh no. She was a very quiet lady—very

charming. I know her health has not been very good, but she didn't look the sort to—to take her own life."

" Did the doctor come often ? "

" Yes."

" I want his address."

She got this for him, and then, at his request, found a specimen of the dead woman's handwriting. It was absolutely identical with that on the note.

" There is an inkwell in the kitchen. Is that usually there ? "

" Sometimes I write my letters there."

" Was that inkwell there this morning—when you left ? "

" I couldn't say for certain."

" Where did Miss Russell usually write her letters ? "

" At the bureau—there."

McLean walked across to the piece of furniture and let down the flap. Inside were ink, pens, paper, and a blotting-pad. It was the blotting-pad that interested him most. Finally he took out the blotting-paper, rolled it up and put it in his pocket.

On the following day he interviewed the dead girl's medical attendant—a Dr. Wingfield. The latter was shocked at hearing the news. He had known the dead woman for some three years, and had attended her for some obscure nervous disorder which was apt to give her blinding headaches. But he had seen her a few days previously and she had appeared quite bright. Better than he had seen her for a long time. He admitted, however, that attacks came on very suddenly.

McLean found the case very interesting, for there were one or two points which put the suicide verdict out of court. The note which had been left had been blotted, yet there was no blotting-paper near it, nor did the blotter in the bureau bear any sign of the message. But the outstanding point of interest lay in the almost certain fact that the key found in the lock of the kitchen door had been turned by some instrument from the other side ! On the end of it were marks which bore this out. Also he could prove that the newspaper wedge found at the bottom of the kitchen door had been inserted from the outside !

At McLean's request the inquest was postponed for a few days. In the meantime the maidservant had telegraphed the dead woman's uncle in Paris, and he had wired back to say he was returning at once. But before he could reach London an unexpected visitor arrived. She was the living image of the dead woman, and gave her name as Mrs. Ongar.

" I am Phyllis's sister," she admitted. " But I was married last year and went to Canada with my husband. We had to come to England unexpectedly, and I intended to take my sister by surprise. The maid sent me to you."

"You must have been twins," said McLean.

"Yes. But this is terrible. She wrote me regularly and her letters were always cheerful. I knew she had been ill, but she never complained."

"You lived in that house before you were married?"

"Yes—with Uncle Theodore."

"You have never known your sister so depressed that she was capable of taking her own life?"

"Never."

McLean went to his desk and produced the note left on the table. He handed it to the visitor, and she wrinkled her brows.

"I should never have dreamed that such a thing could happen. It is incredible."

"I agree. As a matter of fact I have grave doubts that your sister took her own life."

"What do you mean?"

"Please do not press me for an explanation—at the moment. I understand that your uncle and a certain solicitor were joint trustees under the will of your father?"

"That is so."

"You know the terms of that will?"

"Yes. We were to come into the property on attaining the age of twenty-one, but if either of us should marry before then she would forgo her inheritance."

" And you did that ? "

" Yes. I fell in love, and my husband was in a good position. I was quite willing that my sister should enjoy the whole estate."

" What would happen in the event of your sister failing to survive the period ? "

" I—I forget."

" Would your uncle benefit ? "

" I don't think so. It is so long ago I can't recall all the details. But you can find out."

" I intend doing so. In the meantime I want your assistance. It may lead to nothing, but, on the other hand, it may be of the greatest value. I believe your sister was murdered, and in order to establish that I want you to act in a certain way. Are you willing ? "

" It sounds terrible," she said. " But if what you say is true I will do anything in my power to serve the ends of justice."

" Thank you ! Now listen to me."

§

McLean's scheme was a bold one, and a lot of strings had to be pulled before it could be put into operation. He went to the house where the tragedy had taken place and told the maidservant to tell her employer that Inspector McLean wished to see him immediately he arrived. A few hours later McLean was rung up and heard a rather agitated voice at the other end of the line.

"Mr. Theodore Russell speaking. I have just returned from Paris, and am shocked to hear of this terrible tragedy. I understand you wish to see me?"

McLean said that was so, and promised to be at the house within half an hour. When he arrived he found a dark, tall man of about fifty, pacing his drawing-room nervously. He bade McLean take a chair and offered him a cigar, which McLean declined.

"I can't control myself," he said. "It is the last thing in the world that I expected. I oughtn't to have left her in the house alone."

"But there was the maid?"

"The maid. Ah, yes—of course. But she goes out very frequently. On that day she was out all the time. My poor niece was apt to get fits of melancholia. I—I feel almost responsible—for her untimely death."

McLean smiled and shook his head.

"You mustn't say that," he said. "For the simple reason that it has not come to that—yet."

Russell stared at him in amazement.

"What do you mean?"

"Your niece is not dead."

Russell grasped the back of a chair, and for a moment he was absolutely speechless.

"But the doctor said—— The maid heard him. Also I happened to see a paragraph in the newspaper."

"There are occasions when even the cleverest medical men are misled. Your niece is at a nursing home, but still unconscious. She is yet far from being out of danger, but there is a great chance of her reviving."

Russell's face went green. He gulped, passed his hand across his brow and then tried to smile.

"Can—can I see her?" he asked.

"It is possible. Here is the telephone number. You can ring up now."

"Yes—yes."

He put the call through and finally got on to the matron of the nursing home. But upon inquiring in a strangled voice if he could see Miss Russell, he was told that it was out of the question at the moment. The matron would telephone him as soon as the patient recovered consciousness.

"Is—there hope of that?" he asked eagerly.

"Every hope."

"Oh—thank you!"

He uttered a sigh as he hung up the receiver, but it was not exactly a sigh of relief. McLean knew that the murderer was standing before him, but much had to be done before he could prove this. That afternoon he saw the dead girl's twin sister.

" You—you saw him ? " she asked.

" Yes."

" Did he believe you ? "

" There was no alternative. Of course this make-believe cannot go on for long. There must be a coroner's inquest, and that will give the whole show away. I have only a couple of days to prove my theory, and I am not sure that it can be done. Please continue to keep your presence in London a secret. I may yet need you in a desperate venture."

" You think—he—he—killed——? "

" I am sure of it."

She winced, but managed to control her horror. When she left, McLean pondered his next move. He believed that if Russell were to hear that his niece had recovered her senses he would take flight. To McLean it was clear that Russell had made a lightning trip from Paris on the day when he knew that the maidservant was at the wedding of her brother. By some means he had rendered his niece unconscious, placed her in the position in which she had been found, and turned on the gas. Afterwards he had managed to turn the key in the lock by grasping the end of it with some tool, such as a pair of pliers, and wedged paper under the door —from the outside.

But the unsolved portion of the puzzle lay in the

existence of the note, in which the dead girl expressed her intention to take her life. He had had expert advice on the handwriting, and there was no doubt whatever that it was that of the dead woman. Could Russell have induced her to write such a thing before rendering her unconscious? That seemed most improbable. Yet there it was, the damning flaw in his theory, and one not easy to overcome.

Then there was the motive. That too was rather obscure. He had ascertained that in the event of the property not falling to either daughter it would go to Theodore Russell's elder brother, now resident in America. So between Theodore and a small fortune was yet another person thousands of miles away. It was on the following morning that McLean got the motive securely fixed. He watched Theodore leave the house, and then called and inquired for him. The maidservant told him " the master " had just gone out, and McLean entered the place with the professed intention of waiting. But as soon as he was left alone he started investigating. Half an hour later he found something important. It was a telegram in one of Russell's coat pockets, and it ran:

" Regret inform you your brother Maurice passed away to-day after operation.—Alice."

This was dated a week prior to the tragedy, and

McLean was satisfied that Russell's scheme had been born on the receipt of this news. But he yet had to prove that Russell was in London on the day of the tragedy, and that the note was left by him and not by the dead girl.

But in the meantime the coroner was pressing for an inquest, and time was of the utmost importance. When McLean saw Russell again, that worthy manifested singular behaviour. It was as if he suspected a plot of some kind.

"I should like to see my poor niece," he said. "Surely she cannot be unconscious all this time?"

"I believe she is recovering."

"Then I will see her. I insist."

He thereupon rang up the nursing home, and made known his intention. McLean heard him say he would call that afternoon at three o'clock. Half an hour later McLean was closeted with the twin sister.

"I am sorry to have to ask you to do this," he said. "But much hangs upon it. Your uncle suspects a plot. He does not believe the story about the nursing home. When he has reason to believe that my assertions are true, it is my belief he will flee the country. I want that to happen, for it is necessary for me to see his passport, which at the moment cannot be found. He will take it with him."

"But am I to accuse him?"

"No. You must lie quite still, with your eyes closed. You are quite sure he has no means of knowing that you are in England?"

"Quite. We came unexpectedly."

"Good!"

§

Theodore Russell arrived at the nursing home punctually at three o'clock. He was met by the matron, who informed him that his niece was out of danger, but still unable to speak. But he insisted upon seeing her, and ultimately she consented. Looking somewhat puzzled he followed her into a private ward, and there he saw—or thought he saw—the girl he imagined was beyond human aid. McLean had made her up well and she looked as if she had been through a great ordeal.

"Extraordinary!" he gasped.

"She has had a very bad time. For days it has been touch and go with her. Please do not try to speak to her."

Russell gulped. Little beads of perspiration stood out on his forehead. He had not the slightest intention of speaking to her. On the contrary, he dreaded she might come to consciousness and see him.

"I will not stay longer," he said. "Please let me know how she progresses."

On the following morning McLean's prognostication was proved correct. Russell left his house fairly early, carrying a suit-case. McLean followed him to Victoria Station, and arrested him as he was approaching the booking office.

"On what charge?" he demanded.

"The *attempted* murder of your niece—Phyllis Russell."

"But I was in Paris!"

McLean slipped his hand into Russell's inside pocket and secured his passport, the end of which was visible. He opened the book and found what he expected to find—a visa stamped at Dover on the date of the murder. Russell's face went pallid as he realised the seriousness of McLean's discovery.

At Scotland Yard he was placed in a cell, and McLean went to confer with his chief. The Assistant Commissioner was still a little puzzled about the charge.

"Why did you charge him with attempted murder?" he inquired.

"Because he believes his niece is still alive. It is highly probable he will make a statement, because he will realise that if the girl is alive she will accuse him. He has nothing to gain by pleading 'Not guilty.'"

On the following day the inquest was held, and on the strength of McLean's evidence a verdict of "murder" was secured. But the prisoner knew nothing of this. It was now clear to him that his scheme had failed, and during the evening he sent a message to the effect that he wished to make a statement. Brook and McLean went to the cell, and Russell's statement was taken down.

He admitted planning the crime. The telegram announcing his brother's death had tempted him to possess himself of a considerable fortune. He had known that the maidservant was having the day off to attend a wedding, and he had chosen that day as the most suitable. In order to scatter a red-herring across the trail he had pleaded a business appointment in Paris. But he had crossed on the morning of the day of the crime, and reached London late in the afternoon. Phyllis was surprised to see him. A chloroformed handkerchief had rendered her unconscious, and afterwards he had covered his tracks by latching the window and locking the kitchen door by means of a pair of pliers.

"And the note?" queried McLean. "How did you fake that?"

"It was done before I left for Paris. My writing is bad, and at times Phyllis used to copy out my manuscripts for me. I wrote a short story in which a girl committed suicide by putting her head into a gas-oven, and then left a note behind her. I wrote that story purposely, and got Phyllis to make a copy for me. I took the manuscript with me, and brought back only that portion of a sheet containing the message. I had to tear a page in half in order to isolate it from the other material. I found an inkwell and pen, and left the note there to make it look like a genuine suicide. That is all I have to say. Gambling has been my curse. It ruined me and drove me to this. I can't imagine how—how she got over it."

A typed copy was made of the statement, and early the next morning it was given to Russell to sign. He read it and appended his name. Not once did he express his regret. If he had any pity it was for himself.

"Rather clever—the business of the note," mused McLean.

"Not so bad. It was the only way I could get her handwriting. If she hadn't recovered so miraculously you couldn't have charged me."

"I think we could," replied McLean. "As a matter of fact a different charge is to be brought against you."

"What do you mean?"

McLean took a newspaper from his pocket, and handed it to the prisoner. On the front page was a brief account of the inquest and the verdict.

"But—but she didn't die! I saw her with my own eyes."

McLean shook his head.

"You saw her twin sister, who came to London unexpectedly, and in time to assist in clearing up the matter. You can keep the paper."

Russell groaned and his body seemed to crumple up. As McLean left the cell he hurled a torrent of abuse at him.

"Impenitent wretch," said McLean. "Our tears would be wasted on his account. I fancy this statement will ring down the curtain."

McLEAN INVESTIGATES   XI

§

KING DJALMAR'S visit to London was marked with considerable demonstration, for it was the first time that this Eastern monarch had left his small, but politically important, kingdom to see the sights of the outer world, and London was giving him the reception it usually gave to royal visitors. So far Djalmar's promenades had been of an informal character—a few shopping expeditions and a theatre or two—but a big demonstration was soon to take place on a grand style, and flags and other decorations were already being erected along the proposed route.

And it was not only on the surface that excitement was rife. Behind the scenes, in several places, certain officials manifested considerable anxiety over this royal visitor. His little kingdom was a strategical " hot spot," watched over and coveted by various interests, each with an axe to grind, and as a result Djalmar's emergence from his sheltering mountains was fraught with some danger. In Paris a plot against his life had been narrowly frustrated, and now had come London's turn.

McLean's department, among others, was watching the course of events, and working in close connection with the Secret Service. Documents and photographs were constantly being perused, and special information from innumerable sources investigated. One morning McLean received information for his private knowledge. It was in code —and very brief.

"Decode that, Brook," he said. "From 3xx."

Sergeant Brook took the buff slip and referred to the "key." He whistled as he handed the result to McLean. It read:

"GIGOL IN ENGLAND. PROBABLY CROSSED BY AIRPLANE. SOURCE OF INFORMATION UNIMPEACHABLE."

"Hm! That means business," mused McLean. "I have an idea we are going to find our time fully occupied."

"There is a plot then?"

"Never any doubt about that. But the devil of it is to know where to start. Look at those photographs—all supposed to be Gigol. They're as different as any collection of things could be."

He turned over the prints. They portrayed men in various costumes and make-up. The only point of similarity lay in the eyes of each subject—curious, long, deep-set eyes that would hold the attention of any person. The problem of age was insoluble. It might have been anything from twenty-five to forty.

"And we are supposed to locate him among eight million people. A pretty big task, Brook."

"You think the attempt in Paris was instigated by him?"

"The French police are emphatic on that point. But he is a phantom. The master mind behind half a dozen assassinations during the past five years. It's going to be difficult—very difficult."

"Why should he want to kill Djalmar?"

"There are a hundred possible reasons. But one is sufficient—reward. Not a matter of a hundred pounds or so, but vast sums that are commensurate with the danger. To carry out such schemes a big organisation is essential—the assistance of trusted men—desperate men. Gigol has all those at his command. If he is in England it means—real business. What is the date fixed for the procession?"

"The eighteenth."

"Two days."

"You think it will take place then?"

"It may be attempted before that—at any

moment. But two days is the limit, because Djalmar leaves England on the following day."

Brook was of opinion that the big spectacle was the least favourable time for such an attempt to be made, but McLean reasoned differently. The only hope of success in such a hazardous adventure lay in a perfectly organised plan, and that could only be made by the plotters possessing a knowledge of the intended victim's prospective movements. A man did not go out to assassinate a royal personage in any haphazard fashion—unless he were demented. A thousand details had to be worked out in advance. And that was where the fertile brain of the man known as Gigol came in.

McLean conferred with his confrères, and it was agreed that while they should of necessity act in concert, a certain margin of latitude should be given each man until the mysterious Gigol was located. There were in London half a dozen notorious clubs where political plots were hatched, and where desperate characters gathered on occasion. Such places were well known to the police, and were permitted to remain open because they were an aid rather than a hindrance to the law. When McLean left his confrères he had certain definite plans in his mind. To find Gigol in the ordinary way was out of the question. The photographs were practically useless for the purpose of identification. One had to work through second and even third parties. On the following day McLean went to a house in Kensington where resided a one-time international crook named Paley. Paley had given McLean the fight of his life seven years ago, and as a result served five years in prison. He was now a reformed character—due chiefly to the fact that a relative had left him enough money to live a life of ease. In the circumstances he bore McLean no ill-will, and on several occasions had given him information that proved to be of extreme value.

He now welcomed his late enemy effusively, offered him a cigar and a drink—also his most comfortable chair. Paley had got " religion " badly, was interested in the Y.M.C.A., and was at this moment engaged in making a new translation of the Bible.

" It's a year since I saw you last, McLean," he said. " You've gone a long distance since the old days, eh ? When you had me put away for that pleasant vacation you were just a sergeant. What can I do for you, anyway ? "

" Have you ever heard of a man named Gigol ? "

" Gigol ? " Paley stroked his chin reflectively. " Somehow the name seems familiar. Was it in Milan ? No. Gigol—Gigol—where the devil did I hear that name ? "

McLean produced a bundle of photographs and gave them to Paley. Paley turned them over one by one. It was evident he did not recognise any of them, and that he was engaged in trying to recall in what connection he had heard the name. At last his eyes lighted up.

"I've got it! It wasn't in Milan. It was in Rome—1917. I was working with a man named Ferrari. Dirty business it was too, but that doesn't matter now. Ferrari told me he had got into Gigol's clutches—and had been chosen by lot to do a certain job. He funked it at the last and ran for his life. Ultimately he had to clear out of Italy. Gigol had spies everywhere and Ferrari's life wasn't safe there. That's all I know about Gigol. I never came into contact with him myself."

"Where is this man Ferrari?"

"In London. Doing good business in the import trade—Italian comestibles—one of those smelly shops in Soho. I've got his card here—calls himself Mitchell."

He found the card and handed it to McLean. McLean copied the address and an hour later was in the neighbourhood of Soho. It was a simple matter to find Mitchell's business, for it was a large double-fronted shop, full of food-stuffs, and flying the Italian flag. It was on the point of closing, and Mitchell—alias Ferrari—was in his office balancing up his books. Upon mentioning Paley's name McLean was asked to wait, and after a lapse of ten minutes he was shown into the office. The proprietor of the business was a big fellow, with an enormous black moustache, curled up at the ends. His prosperity simply oozed from him.

"You know my old friend Paley?" he inquired.

"Oh yes. I have just left him. I am interested in a man named Gigol——"

"Gigol!" Ferrari's fat hands closed and trembled. "What—what do you know of Gigol?"

"Nothing. That is why I have come to you. You could help me very much by telling me what you know about him."

Ferrari waved a fat finger warningly.

"Have nothing to do with him, my friend. He is the devil. I have reason to know that."

"But I want to get into touch with him."

"Then you are mad. It is all very well here, in London, to talk of Gigol, but in Italy—in the slums of Naples that name has a different meaning. And not only in Naples, but in Berlin, Paris, Warsaw—you have but to mention Gigol——"

"I am anxious to meet him, but I want to meet him here, in London."

"But it is——"

McLean projected his head forward.

"Gigol is in London at this moment."

"What!"

Ferrari sat down heavily in a chair that was immediately behind him, and his terror was marked clearly on his expansive face.

"It seems to perturb you, Mr. Mitchell?"

" My God ! Oh, no—no—it is years ago. But who are you ? Why do you want to meet that—that fiend ? "

" Merely to help—certain people."

" Leave him alone ! I tell you he is powerful—even here. For years he has treated the police forces of all countries with contempt. Around him he has a band of desperate, well-paid assassins, and——"

" It sounds interesting. Have you any idea where I might possibly find him ? "

" No. At least——"

" Go on."

" Well, there is a night club in Islington called the ' Peacocks ' which is frequented by persons in touch with Gigol. I have never been there because——" His eyes shifted nervously. " You can gain admittance by proffering three lire—that is the recognised password."

" They are all Italians ? "

" Oh no—all nationalities. You do not speak Italian ? "

" Only a few words. But my French is pretty good."

" That would do. But I warn you it is dangerous to get mixed up with Gigol's affairs."

" What is he like—to look at ? "

" I only saw him once—a young man. He would be older now—probably about thirty-five. Handsome, on the short side, with eyes that seem to bore into you."

"I have some photographs here. Look at them!"

Ferrari examined the prints, and admitted that any of them might be Gigol.

"It is hard to say," he said. "I have heard he is a master at disguise—and a born actor. My advice to you is to have nothing to do with him."

McLean thanked him, and ultimately left him, after ascertaining the address of the club. It was now nearly eight o'clock, and he decided to lose no time in making an attempt to get into touch with Gigol. Ten o'clock found him in Islington, garbed to look like a rather down and out foreigner, and with a very useful weapon concealed in his hip pocket. The club was a suite of rooms over a large furniture shop, and entry was made through a small vestibule where a lantern-jawed foreigner played the part of hall-porter. McLean lounged in and displayed his three lire pieces. He was scrutinised and let pass.

§

The main room of the club was a combined café and dance-hall. The tables were scattered along either side, and the centre portion was given over to dancing. By eleven o'clock the place was fairly well patronised. On the surface it appeared to be quite a respectable club. Its habitués were on the whole well-dressed, and well-behaved. There was no sign of drunkenness, and the dancing was on a much higher level than in most places of that type. The men were in the majority, and were as mixed as any collection of men could be. Some were dancing, some sitting in groups of twos and threes, and a few were sitting alone.

McLean tried to get into conversation with one fellow, but received the cold shoulder. He tried again in another quarter with no better result. Half an hour later a woman entered, alone. She was simply dressed, and carried herself with an air of perfect self-possession. Her type was an interesting one, and McLean could quite imagine her in the rôle of a decoy—or in any adventure that called for courage and self-reliance. She took a seat quite close to him and ordered a coffee and milk. After some minutes her eyes found his, and he took the opportunity to make some casual remark about the weather—in French.

" You are French ? " she asked.

" Yes—Provence."

" Ah—a beautiful place."

" You know it ? "

" Very well. You do not come here often ? "

" This is my first visit. I was introduced by a friend—a man named Jules Villon."

It was a happy shot. McLean remembered that

name. Villon had been arrested in Paris on a charge of espionage, and sentenced to five years' penal servitude. At the trial it was proved that Villon was an international spy, and mixed up with various secret organisations.

"I seem to recall the name," she said.

"Quite likely. Jules was most—unfortunate. There was a prospect of my having to leave France, and he told me to come here."

She smiled and displayed a perfect set of white teeth.

"For convivial company?"

"Scarcely. The fact is, I—I am looking for something to do."

"But this is not an employment bureau!"

He smiled and gazed at the dancers and the lounging parties. Opposite there was a little quartet of men who seemed to be engaged in very earnest conversation. One of them had a plan or map spread out before him and constantly referred to it. McLean was interested in them, and was anxious to get within earshot.

"Do you dance?" he asked boldly.

"A little."

"It's rather a good band. Shall we?"

She nodded, and he followed her into the open space. In a few moments they were dancing together, to the latest Charleston. McLean found her a past master in the art. All her movements were finished—perfect. As they passed the sitting group of men he contrived to catch a glimpse of the plan. It was a large-scale map of London, and various thoroughfares were marked in red. The big bulk of St. Paul's Cathedral stood out plainly, close to one of the red markings, and he knew that what he saw was the route to be taken by the procession. But he heard no conversation, for his beautiful partner seemed to display a desire to leave that part of the room. At last the music ended and they sat down.

" Thank you ! " she said. " That was delightful. You did not tell me your name ? "

" Does it matter ? "

" Well—no."

" All the same I will tell you. It is Georges Laudac."

" A good name. Mine is Beatrice d'Annunciata, and I come from Venice. Now we are formally introduced. You do not understand the Italian tongue ? "

" No," he lied.

" Ah—that is a pity ! "

" I realise it now. Beatrice d'Annunciata ! It is like music itself."

" Ah, you have the flattering tongue of the born Frenchman."

McLean appeared to be cool and unobservant, but all the time his attention was riveted on the men with the plan. A minute or two later one of them consulted the clock and the whole party rose and made to go. McLean too looked at the clock and gave a start.

"Mon Dieu! It is nearly midnight, and I have to see a friend in ten minutes. I beg you to excuse me, Signorita."

She did so gracefully, expressing the hope that she might see him again soon.

"To-morrow night—at the same time—here?"

"Yes."

He bowed and left the place. Immediately she rose and went across to the four men who were just about to depart. Her eyes flashed fire as she confronted them.

"You fools to talk here—and display that plan. That man was watching you. If Gigol knew——"

"Gigol! What do you know of Gigol?"

"I came here to watch you. Go now! He is expecting you. And remember not to visit this place again—until the thing is done. Hurry!"

The man with the plan scowled, but it was clear that he was terrified. In a few moments they had gone, and Beatrice d'Annunciata was not long in following their example.

McLean had hidden up in a passage on the opposite side of the road, and as soon as the men appeared he commenced to stalk them. They were evidently looking for a taxi, but it was some time before they found one. McLean had to act like lightning in order not to lose them, and he was only just in time. Nipping into a taxi he pointed to the disappearing light of the other vehicle.

"Keep that taxi in sight," he said. "But don't overtake it."

The driver was a man of some intelligence and the chase went on for a considerable time. It finished in the neighbourhood of Paddington. McLean saw the leading taxi pull up outside a large house, standing back from the avenue through which they were passing.

"Pull up round the next turning," he said.

Before the taxi was at rest he was on the pavement, giving a ten-shilling note to the grateful driver. Then he slipped into the avenue and watched the four men enter the house on the opposite side of the road. The door closed after them and McLean approached it. There was a light in the hall, but the basement appeared to be in darkness. He decided to attempt to gain entry that way, and descended into the area. It was a simple matter to force the latch of one of the windows, and in a minute or two he was inside the building. Using a pocket torch he made his way upstairs. Here he came upon the domestic quarters, which had evidently been moved up when the house was modernised. He avoided them and slipped along a passage, to where he could hear the low murmur of men's voices. Ultimately he discovered the source of the sound—a room lying on his right. He was loitering there when the stairs creaked and conveyed to him the fact that someone was descending. Instantly he concealed himself behind a large coat-rack beyond the door.

Five seconds later a figure approached him. The light was at the back of it and he could not see the face clearly, but as it approached the door a black mask was slipped over the indistinct face. It was a man in evening dress—fairly short, but young judging from his walk. A cigarette was between his lips, and he halted and listened for a moment before he entered the room where his confederates were waiting. That it was Gigol, McLean had no doubt.

He approached the door and listened intently. A gruff voice was speaking, in Italian, and as a result McLean missed about fifty per cent. of what was said.

" The work is finished . . . no inquiries of any kind. . . . Peter says . . . the circuit has been tested . . . dynamite. . . ."

A youthful, musical voice broke in :

" You are sure the wiring is completely hidden ? "

" Absolutely. No one would suspect. . . . The procession leaves the House of Commons at eleven o'clock. It should reach the bell at about eleven-thirty—or a quarter to twelve. . . . We have arranged for Peter to leave by the side exit, and shall have the car on the Embankment ready for him."

"Good! But there must be no mistake. Can Peter see the procession before it reaches Fleet——?"

McLean heard no more, for there was a sudden noise away to his right, and he turned to see a man-servant gazing at him in bewilderment.

"Help! Signor——!"

The strident voice set the house echoing before McLean could still it. He whipped out his pistol and made a leap towards the front door, but instantly the crowd from the room were on his heels.

"Stop! Halt—or you are a dead man!"

He gave one glance over his shoulder, and realised that this might be no exaggeration. The man in the black mask had a pistol levelled at him, and there were two other fire-arms exposed behind the pistol. McLean was nothing if not discreet.

"Ah—Signor Gigol!" he said.

"You have the advantage," said the calm voice. "I will trouble you to throw down that pistol."

McLean pitched the weapon forward. He was in a tight corner and was well aware of it. That these men were desperate was plain enough. It was six against one—impossible odds.

" Search him, Tomasso ! "

The big man ran his hands over McLean's pockets, but found nothing but the electric torch, a knife, a cigarette-case and an automatic cigarette-lighter. The knife was taken, but the other articles were left.

" Bring him inside ! "

McLean was compelled to enter the room in which the conversation had taken place. Gigol sat on the end of the table—a graceful, attractive figure. His dark eyes held a strange lustre—behind the mask.

" What is your business here ? " he asked calmly. " In whose employ are you ? "

McLean shook his head. It was evident to him that Tomasso recognised him as the recent visitor to the " Peacocks " club, but he preferred not to mention it. Gigol repeated his question—a little more tensely.

" I was merely—interested," said McLean. " With your permission I will retire."

Gigol laughed amusedly.

" A humorist—eh ? Well, *I* may amuse *you* before we have finished. Tomasso, and you, Paul, bring him below. You other two make sure he has no friends outside. Hurry ! "

McLean was escorted into the basement, and flung into what appeared to be an empty coal-hole. There he was bound hand and foot, and gagged with a filthy rag. Then the door was closed on him and he heard two bolts pushed home.

§

To McLean the night was one long agony. The place was practically airless, and there were rats. So tight were the bonds round his legs that they impeded the blood circulation and caused a sensation of faintness. He blamed himself for getting into this mess—his fondness for working alone. Yet most of his successes had been achieved that way, and it was obvious that he would have missed learning what he had learnt had he not followed the taxi and taken the risk of entering the house.

The bell . . . Fleet Street! Then the word "dynamite." It meant that all their fell plans were laid. Somewhere in the neighbourhood of Fleet Street, death was waiting a royal personage, and he had sufficient appreciation of the mysterious Gigol to credit him with the ability to avoid making mistakes. But why dynamite? That was an unusual explosive to use! And the business of wiring?

Hours passed and a grey light filtered through a grating into his cell. Morning had arrived. A few more hours and the procession would be leaving the House of Commons. Naturally it would be well guarded, but that would not help. The danger was real. Something must be done!

He twisted and turned, and at last managed to move the bandage that kept the gag in place. Then he rid himself of the gag, and breathed a little more freely. Moreover, his brain became clearer. There was the small grating overhead, but he did not know whether it led to a public thoroughfare, and even if it did he had no means of writing a note for help. To use his voice would merely bring someone down to re-gag him.

One of his hands came into contact with a small protuberance inside his vest pocket. It was the small petrol cigarette-lighter, and it gave him an idea. But to get hold of it meant another long series of twists and painful convulsions. At last he managed to get the implement between his fingers. A slight pressure and the cap flew back, exposing the wick and the wheel and flint. Click! A flash—and no result. After four attempts the wick caught fire. He held it close to the rope that bound his arms and watched the stout hemp smoulder. . . . At last a strand came apart, then another. His arms were free! He turned his attention to his numbed legs. When the knots were untied he could scarcely move his limbs. It took ten minutes of massage to get any real "feeling" into them. He stood up, with new hope in his breast.

The next move was problematical. He tried the door, but it was as solid as iron. Then the grating—but that was equally impossible to move. It was obvious that the only way out was by some stratagem. Filling his lungs with air he put up a tremendous shout. Again and again his cry for help rose stentoriously, and at last it had effect. There was a sound from without. A bolt was drawn and then another. The door opened slowly and an arm came round it, carrying a pistol. McLean dived at it, bent the wrist with a powerful movement and possessed himself of the weapon. The next moment he was outside and face to face with the man-servant.

"Get inside!" he said. "Quick!"

The fellow retreated backwards and McLean accelerated the movement, and slammed the door on him, bolting it as before. He made his way up the stairs, a blackened, awful-looking figure—ready for any emergency. The place was quiet, and when he reached the hall he saw the time—10.30!

Time was now of the utmost importance. He remembered having seen a telephone in the room on his right. Opening the door cautiously he entered. It was then he suffered a surprise. Seated at a table writing was a woman—the woman he had met at the night club—the beautiful Beatrice d'Annunciata. In a moment he realised the truth. She was Gigol! Gigol was a woman!

"Ah!" he said. "So we *do* meet again, Signorita Gigol!"

There was a lightning movement and the flash of a fire-arm. A bullet whistled past his head. He held his fire but advanced on her with a chair extended in his left hand. A second shot ripped through the wooden bottom. He pinned her to the wall between the four legs and put the pistol near her breast.

"Drop that weapon or I shall fire. I mean it!"

But she was as undaunted as ever. He raised the chair slightly and pinned her arm against the wall with one of the square legs. The pistol dropped, and he picked it up.

"Stay there!" he said. "I advise you not to move."

He went to the telephone, and used it, still facing her. Scotland Yard was connected and in a few seconds he was talking to Brook.

"McLean speaking. The procession must be delayed until we have time to investigate. There is a big plot to assassinate—somewhere in Fleet Street——"

Brook interrupted to say that the procession had already started and that it was a quarter-past eleven. McLean gasped and a laugh came from his prisoner.

"You are a little late, my dear Inspector. The clock in the hall is slow."

"Hello, Brook!" bawled McLean. "I've got Gigol here—No. 24 Eglinton Avenue, Paddington,

I'm going to lock her—yes, *her*—in the coal-cellar downstairs. Can't wait a moment. Come here at once in the fast car and then go to the Embankment Gardens. Hurry! This is touch and go."

He put down the receiver, and advanced on the woman. There was no fear in that face—just contempt. He could not help but admire her courage.

"Where is this thing to take place?" he demanded.

"I thought you knew. You are so clever."

"You refuse to tell?"

She shrugged her shoulders, and he gripped her by the arm and led her away hastily. In the passage she turned and made a violent attempt to escape, but was overpowered and impelled down the basement stairs. McLean opened the door of the coal-cellar and pushed her inside, bolting the door after her. There was no time to bind her, and he realised there was a risk of her escaping with the aid of the man-servant. But every moment was precious, and he had no alternative to leaving things chance in that respect.

A minute later he was running down the avenue, searching for a taxi. The first one he saw carried a passenger. He stood in its path and bundled the indignant man outside.

"Police service," he explained to the driver. "Drive like the devil to Fleet Street——"

" Can't get there———"

" I know. Put me down as near as you can to the Temple. Do you know any place called ' The Bell ' ? "

" No."

" Never mind—hurry ! "

He was whirled through the streets at an appalling rate, and ultimately reached the congested crowd at the bottom of Kingsway. From a distance he could hear the sound of a band, and cheering. To divert the procession was out of the question now. His only chance was to find the place mentioned—" The Bell."

Running at the rear of the packed spectators he reached the commencement of Fleet Street. There he was wedged tight for a few seconds. While he fought to get free his eyes lighted on a significant thing. It was a huge floral bell suspended over the centre of the street on a wire which went across to either side. On the left side the wire finished at a standard, but on the opposite side it appeared to go through the window on the first floor, and as he looked he saw a man's head projected from the window—gazing towards the approaching procession.

The bell ! He saw it all now. That innocent-looking decoration, bearing the word " Welcome," contained an instrument of death. The wire which carried it was an electric cable connected up with a switch and battery inside the room opposite. Dynamite! Yes, dynamite struck downwards!

He fought to get to the other side of the road, and was cursed roundly by more than one spectator. All the time the procession was getting closer to the fatal spot. At last he broke through, but came up against a policeman. By a stroke of good luck McLean recognised the officer, and the latter gazed at the begrimed figure in amazement.

"Inspector Mc——!"

"Get me through that crowd," said McLean. "There's danger here. Hurry, man!"

The burly constable saw him across the road and the crowd made way. He found a side entrance to the room above the shop and ran up the stairs. At the top was a door—locked. He tapped lightly.

"Who is there?"

"Gigol," he replied. "Open quick!"

The door opened a few inches and a dark face came to view. Instantly McLean pushed his pistol into the astonished man's chest.

"Get back!"

He entered the room and drove the man into the corner. The place contained nothing but a table and a chair, and on the table was a small box with a switch on the side. McLean saw a wire making contact with the box.

"Stand away!" he cried.

There was a great cheer from outside the window,

and McLean caught a glimpse of some mounted troops and then the royal coach. The man moved suddenly to the switch, desperate to the last moment. McLean fired and the big body pivoted and fell. In a moment the connecting wire was broken, and McLean went to the window. His friend, the constable, had heard the shot above the cheering, and was looking up. McLean beckoned him, and saw the rear part of the royal coach disappearing. He uttered a sigh of tremendous relief and turned to the wounded man. His injury was comparatively slight and he was handed over to the constable.

"Take him along," said McLean. "We haven't finished yet."

Along the Embankment Brook was waiting, having performed miracles in the way of rapid transport. Ten minutes later four other men were arrested—in a waiting car.

"Did you get Gigol?" inquired McLean.

"You bet," replied Brook with some pride. "Some woman that! Hark at 'em cheering back there! Lord, if they only knew!"

That evening a gang of experts removed the bell, and it was detonated in a wide field. Before he left England, King Djalmar's equerry dispatched a token of his royal master's gratitude to McLean, while Signorita Beatrice d'Annunciata sat in a very confined space, awaiting what was coming to her.

McLEAN INVESTIGATES XII

SERGEANT BROOK had been to Muswell Hill in response to an urgent request from a Mr. Julius Singer, who had telephoned overnight in a state of considerable agitation. He arrived back at noon and had just finished typing his report when McLean came in from lunch.

" So you're back, Brook ? "

" An hour ago. Another threat case. Took a long time to get a coherent statement. This is it."

McLean perused the typed document. It gave the name of the complainant as Julius Singer, British nationality, a retired merchant from Japan—aged fifty years.

" So he suspects a plot on his life. Motive ? Ah, it's here ! An old quarrel dating back ten years, in connection with pearls. The intending avenger a pearl-diver named Myoto Kaminsu. Letter received July 27 from Paris. You have this letter ? "

Brook handed it to him. It was written in Japanese, but underneath was a translation. It ran, " Did you think Myoto had forgotten ? He comes to avenge his brother on the two dogs who robbed him and sent him to his death."

" Crisp and to the point," mused McLean. " But he mentions two men ? "

"Julius was in business with his brother, Henry. They retired together. Henry now lives in Barnet. I went to see him to find out if he had also been threatened. He said he had not, and was rather inclined to treat the threat with contempt."

"Did he refer to this old quarrel?"

"Yes, but he wouldn't give me any details. I deduced there had been some dirty work, and that Myoto and his brother were left holding the baby. Anyway, Myoto's brother committed hari-kari soon after. The Singers came straight to England."

"Julius takes the threat seriously?"

"Very. He was nervy—jumpy. Carries an automatic, and looks capable of using it."

"What does he expect us to do?"

"Nothing; but if the worst should happen he doesn't want the Jap to get away with it."

"Hm!"

McLean read the latter part of the statement. It gave a description of Myoto—very short, but wiry; a scar in the shape of a cross on his left cheek. Characteristic Mongolian type. Speaks broken English.

"We will institute inquiries at the ports," said McLean. "But most of these threats never materialise."

A few days later it was proved that Myoto had arrived in England. McLean had the train met at Victoria, but the Jap had disappeared. It looked as if he had received warning of being shadowed and had left the train at the last moment at Dover. McLean was a little disappointed and decided to await developments—if any.

He had not long to wait. Within three days a telephone message came to say that a Mr. Singer had been found brutally murdered at his house in Barnet.

"Barnet!" ejaculated Brook. "Then it must be Henry and not Julius. That's a surprise."

"We'll get along there."

They arrived at the house and found Mrs. Singer in tears. It was seven o'clock in the evening, and she had just returned from a bridge drive. She was a woman of about forty, extremely well-preserved, and good-looking.

"Have you called a doctor?" asked McLean.

"Yes. He is with my poor husband now."

She showed McLean and Brook into the sitting-room, where the doctor was found leaning over an inert form striving to induce life into it. He rose as the two officers entered.

"Hopeless, I'm afraid. You are police officers?"

"Yes. Is he dead?"

"Not quite. But he can't last more than a few minutes."

McLean drew closer. Singer was lying on the rug close to the fireplace, with a deep wound in his chest. There had evidently been a great struggle, for his collar was torn off and his throat was bruised and bleeding. A chair close by was overturned, and the carpet disarranged at the corner. The window nearest the fireplace was open at the bottom, and between it and the fireplace were several spots of blood.

Suddenly the mortally wounded man groaned and opened his eyes. The doctor flew to his side. It was clear that death was close upon him, and that he was trying to say something. At last it came—broken and very faint.

"It—it—was—My——"

A rattle in the throat caused the wife to utter a little cry. The next moment the eyes were staring fixedly.

"Gone!"

"Myoto," said Brook. "Then it wasn't bluff after all!"

McLean questioned Mrs. Singer. She had left home at half-past two, leaving a maid and her husband in the house. The maid was due to go out at six o'clock, and apparently had done so. She knew nothing about Myoto, for she had only been married five years, and her husband had never spoken much about his past life, nor had her brother-in-law.

The doctor gave it as his opinion that the wound had been inflicted about a quarter of an hour before he arrived—that would be at six-thirty. He had been rung up by Mrs. Singer. Half an hour later McLean was successful in finding the instrument that had been used. It was a long-bladed Japanese knife, and it was lying in some fairly long grass twenty yards from the open window. There was blood on the handle, but no finger-prints.

"A gloved hand," mused McLean.

McLean left the place soon after the body was removed, but he called again later in the evening to interrogate the maid. She stated she had left her master in the sitting-room at six o'clock, reading a book. There had been no telephone call, nor did she see any person loitering about the house. It was obvious that she knew nothing whatever about the crime and that it would be waste of time to question her further. McLean was about to leave when the brother of the dead man called.

"I got your message, Mona," he said to the pallid widow. "This is terrible! I was at my club——"

He stopped as he saw McLean.

"This is Inspector McLean from Scotland Yard," said Mrs. Singer. "Inspector, my brother-in-law —Mr. Julius Singer."

The visitor bowed. He was greatly shaken. He knew something was going to happen, but expected an attempt would be made upon himself in the first place.

"I informed the police," he said. "I warned them. It is that devil Myoto——"

"That is what he said," interrupted Mrs. Singer. "Who is Myoto—and why should he want to kill my poor husband?"

Singer blinked at this.

"Did Henry live long enough to name his murderer?" he asked.

"Yes. He tried to say Myoto—I heard him. Julius, why didn't you tell me there was a plot to kill him? I had the right to know."

"I—it was an old business. Oh, God, what am I to do? I can't go back to that house. He is waiting for me. He swore he would get—both of us."

"I will have the house watched," said McLean. "You have nothing to fear."

"No—no. I couldn't sleep there. Can—can I see my brother?"

"He has been taken away. Mr. Singer, have you ever seen a knife like this before?"

McLean produced the lethal weapon and Singer started.

"It must be Myoto's. It is the type of knife that pearl-divers use to fight the sharks that sometimes attack them. Was the murder done with—that?"

"Presumably."

"Horrible!" He sank into a chair and wiped

his forehead with a silk handkerchief. McLean questioned him about the past, and he gave a rather unconvincing version of what had taken place. It was evident he was trying to hide up a piece of trickery and robbery, and to make out that Myoto was misled.

"We treated him and his brother quite well," he said. "But he was a man who nurtured grievances. His brother was a gambler and lost his pearls that way. He was under the influence of opium and imagined we robbed him."

"Has he ever threatened you before?"

"Yes. Just before we came to England. I believe an attempt was made on my brother's life in Singapore. But since we have been in England we have heard nothing from Myoto—until a few days ago when the letter came from Paris."

"You cannot swear that this is Myoto's knife?"

"No. I can only say that I have seen him with such a knife in his girdle."

"That is all I have to say at the moment. Do you intend going back to your house?"

Singer wrung his hands in perplexity.

"Shall—shall I be protected?"

"I will see that a man is sent there immediately."

"Then—then I will return—in half an hour's time. Thank you so much, Inspector."

McLean left them together and went back to the

office, with the only exhibit discovered so far. Brook was still there when he arrived.

"Any further luck, sir?"

"No. The brother of the murdered man turned up. He is afraid to go home. I have promised him protection. See that a man is stationed outside his house. Our next job is to find Myoto."

§

The search for Myoto was vain for some days. Both in London and in the provinces the police were busy instituting inquiries at hotels and boarding houses. Several Japanese were apprehended, but all succeeded in clearing themselves.

"Blooming phantom!" grumbled Brook. "And all these Japs are so much alike they might as well be twins—turned out by a machine. I've seen eighteen since yesterday morning."

"He'll turn up sooner or later," said McLean hopefully. "Is that man still watching Singer's house?"

"Yes. Nothing doing there. He's evidently lying quiet for a bit."

A week passed, and then came information from Hornsey to the effect that a Japanese named Myoto Kaminsu was living in a furnished apartment there. A detective had seen him at close quarters and he bore the scar mentioned by Julius Singer. He was still under observation and the Superintendent wished to know if he should apprehend him? McLean said he would prefer to do that himself, and at once went off with Brook.

Ultimately they were taken to the house where the suspected man was living, and found a detective in the vicinity. Myoto had left half an hour ago, and a second detective was shadowing him, but it was his custom to return home round about one o'clock. It was now past twelve, so McLean and Brook loitered near the house. At ten minutes to one Myoto appeared. The three men passed him in the street and McLean caught a glimpse of the scar.

"Our man undoubtedly," he said. "We will give him time to get indoors."

From the corner of the street they saw Myoto enter the house, and almost immediately McLean and Brook retraced their steps and rang the bell. A maid answered it.

"Mr. Myoto Kaminsu?"

"Second floor, sir."

"Thank you. He is expecting us."

On the second floor was a door bearing a visiting card, with Myoto's name on it. McLean wrinkled his brows.

"Rather impudent that!"

"Perhaps he forgot it."

"Hm! A bold customer!"

He pushed the bell and in a few moments the door was opened. The little Jap stood before them—a quaint, diminutive figure with jet-black eyes. He looked scarcely the type of man to deal with a big fellow like the deceased, but in this case it was not wise to judge from outward appearance.

"We are police officers," said McLean. "And we should like a few words with you."

"You will please come inside. I speak small English. Maybe you excuse?"

They entered the flat, and Myoto waved them into chairs. He seemed to be calm enough—merely curious.

"Where were you on August the third—between six and seven o'clock in the evening?" inquired McLean.

"I look."

He referred to a small diary, which he produced from his inner pocket.

"Go to see friend at Wimbledon," he explained. "Leave home at half-past five, but friend he call away. I come back here soon after seven o'clock and read a book."

"So you did not see your friend?"

"No. Call at house, but no one answer."

"Then how do you know he was called away?"

"I write to him afterwards and he tell me."

The answer came very pat. Either Myoto was telling the truth or he was an accomplished liar.

"You knew a man named Singer?"

Myoto's eyes blazed at the mention of the name.

"Long ago I know him, and his brother."

"You had reason to hate them?"

"Yes."

"And recently you wrote Julius Singer a letter from Paris, threatening his life?"

"No. I write him a note to frighten him. I find his address one day in a telephone book while I look for another. Myoto have no intention to take his life."

"Nor his brother's?"

Myoto shook his head emphatically.

"That was simply a foolish threat?"

"Yes."

"Do you know that his brother—Henry Singer—was murdered on the evening of August 3?"

Myoto opened his narrow eyes as wide as possible, and then shook his head.

"No read English. Speak it a little, but no read. I did not know."

"Well, take a look at this." McLean produced the knife. "Have you ever seen this weapon before?"

The Jap's eyes gleamed as they became focussed on the instrument. For a few seconds he was silent.

"It is a diver's knife," he said ultimately. "Myoto see many like that."

"You deny that this knife belonged to you?"

"Yes. I do no diving for many years. Heart go very bad and no able to dive."

"Why did you come to Europe?"

"Learn to speak French and English. I have big store now in Tokyo. Every day I go to English class."

McLean was experiencing considerable doubt. The evidence against Myoto was not very strong, and yet he had written that incriminating letter, in the face of which his explanation sounded thin and unconvincing. To prove that the knife belonged to Myoto was a matter of extreme difficulty. There was another point too, which McLean's keen eyes had detected, and he decided to test his suspicions.

"Is there a pen here?" he asked.

Myoto nodded towards a bureau.

"I want you to write your name—in Japanese characters."

Myoto went to the bureau, took the pen in his left hand and did as he was bid. McLean examined the result and pocketed the sheet of paper.

"That is all I need at the moment," he said.

Brook scratched his chin as they left the house. For the life of him he could not see why McLean had not made an arrest, for he had undoubtedly come with that intention.

"You're puzzled, Brook?"

"Well, I thought it was a clear case."

"Far from it. Myoto never did that job."

Brook was reluctant to argue the point with his superior officer, but it was obvious he held quite a different opinion.

"Will that signature help?" he asked.

"It has done its work."

On the following day McLean was annoyed to find that Superintendent Spalding had gone over his head. Spalding had a nasty habit of interfering in cases where he imagined his knowledge and longer experience were superior to McLean's.

"I arrested Myoto last night," he said. "It wasn't wise to give him too much rope. It should have been done before."

"Was he handcuffed?"

"There was no need. He came quietly."

"He would."

"What do you mean?"

"He can prove his innocence at any moment, and he may defer doing so until after he is charged. Then he will have a splendid case against us."

Spalding smiled in superior fashion.

"The note will convict him. No sensible jury will believe his story. That visit to Wimbledon—he has no means of proving he went there. And the last words of the murdered man. He gave the name of his murderer. You are a trifle too cautious, McLean."

"You intend to charge him?"

"Yes. He comes up to-day."

"Will you bring him here now?"

"For what purpose?"

"I should like to prove to you that he is innocent."

"How?"

"You will see."

"Very well. I will send for him."

Myoto was brought into the Superintendent's office. He was very composed, and smiled as he faced the two men. There was an attaché case on a chair by the window. McLean pointed to it.

"Will you bring that case to me, Mr. Kaminsu?"

The prisoner hesitated and then walked across to the case. He put out his left arm.

"No, the other arm!"

The prisoner remained inactive, and then came back.

"I—I can't," he said.

The Superintendent looked at the hanging right arm, and the truth suddenly burst on him.

"Paralysed!"

The prisoner nodded and twisted his lips. McLean smiled and told the warder to take him away.

"The man who murdered Singer was a fit man," said McLean. "There was a terrible struggle before the knife got home. Myoto could never have done it."

Spalding bit his lip in vexation.

"It's a sham," he said. "I'll have him medically examined. Besides, the murdered man gave the name——"

"He didn't," interrupted McLean. "At least he didn't give Myoto's name. I thought so until I discovered the truth. Now I know what Henry Singer was trying to tell us."

§

Myoto's affliction was found to be genuine, and in the face of it the charge had to be abandoned. Before he left he admitted that he was incensed by the action of the police, and deliberately concealed his physical infirmity. Superintendent Spalding suffered a very natural embarrassment.

McLean was now on a new tack. He visited the house of the dead man while Mrs. Singer was away, and there he found a bundle of letters tied up with pink ribbon. They were from Julius Singer to his brother's wife, and were as passionate as love-letters could be. They begged her to leave a life of misery and disillusion and go with him to Australia.

The writer's house was visited in due course, but there no letters were found. Julius was, presumably, more discreet than the woman he loved. The maid was interrogated, and to McLean's great joy she identified the knife. She had seen it in an old trunk upstairs in the box-room.

" When did you see it last ? "

" About a fortnight ago, when I had occasion to go there."

" Where is your master now ? "

" I don't know. He went out this morning, and said he would return to dinner."

" I want you to say nothing of my visit. It is most important—you understand ? "

" Y-yes," she quavered.

That evening a telegram came to inform the maid that Singer would not be home until the following day. It was handed in at Brighton. Also, by a coincidence, the widow of Henry Singer did not put in an appearance.

" Brook, we are going to Brighton," said McLean. " This time there should be no mistake."

" You have found the murderer ? "

" I think so."

At Brighton the whole evening was spent in trying to trace the wanted man, but his name did not appear in any of the hotel registers. It was obvious that he was using an assumed name.

" That means that the woman is here too," said McLean.

" Is it Julius ? "

" Yes."

" And—the widow ? "

"You have it."

"Well, I'm—— !"

It was at eleven o'clock the next morning that McLean and Brook set eyes on Julius Singer. He was walking towards Black Rock with his sister-in-law.

"We'll get them further along," said McLean, "and cut through the back of the town to avoid the crowds."

They followed the strolling couple, and finally overtook them in a quiet spot by the cliff edge. McLean stepped forward and clapped his hand on Singer's shoulder. The face came round, and alarm entered the eyes for a brief moment. Then Singer smiled.

"Inspector McLean!" he said. "Quite a surprise!"

"I am going to arrest you for the murder of your brother on the evening of August the third," said McLean. "And I must warn you that anything——"

"You—— !"

"Will you come quietly or——?"

Singer's face became convulsed.

"Wait!" he said. "This is nonsense. You were present when my poor brother gave the name of his murderer and——"

"That is one of the reasons why I am arresting you," cut in McLean.

"But he said it was Myo——!"

McLean shook his head.

"He never got as far as that. What he was trying to say was, ' it was *my brother.*' And I have every reason to believe it."

Singer was gasping for breath. He seemed to realise the game was up, and as Brook approached him he made a dive for the cliff edge, but McLean caught him by the coat and held him. The next moment he was a prisoner, with one wrist firmly secured to Brook. McLean turned to the almost fainting woman.

"I want you too, Mrs. Singer."

"I—I am innocent," she wailed.

"That you must endeavour to prove later. Come!"

Three months later Julius Singer was executed, and the pretty widow started to serve a sentence of twelve weary years.

"Love is a curious thing, Brook," drawled McLean. "It can bring heaven to earth, but on the other hand it can also raise hell."

McLEAN INVESTIGATES — XIII

§

THE robbery at the house of Sir Wilfred Dyson was marked with several baffling features. In the first place there was the mystery as to how the house was entered, for after the discovery of the robbery every door had been found locked and bolted on the inside, and all the windows were securely fastened. To add further bewilderment, a quantity of green feathers was found scattered about the room in which the actual theft took place—Lady Dyson's bedroom. These feathers were stuck in vases, pinned to curtains, attached to the four bedposts and arrayed behind pictures like holly at Christmastide.

There was but one object missing, and that was of considerable value. It was a trinket box containing a pearl necklace, several diamond brooches, and a bracelet. This had been kept in a drawer in the wardrobe, which by a strange oversight was not locked. On the night of the robbery both Sir Wilfred and Lady Dyson were out of town, and only the butler and three servants were in the house. None of these had heard a sound.

McLean examined the room carefully, but failed to discover any finger-prints. Upon going to the window he noticed an inscription on the glass. It was the initials O.L. scratched on the glass on the outside, in quite small characters. He called the maid and inquired if she had seen the marks before. She said she had not, and was quite certain they were not there on the preceding day. Later Lady Dyson returned and bore out the maid's statement.

" My—my trinket box has gone ? "

"I am afraid so. Do those initials convey anything to you?"

"Nothing at all. But where did these green feathers come from?"

"They were apparently left by the robber, but with what object remains to be discovered."

"How strange!"

"It appears that your wardrobe was not locked?"

"I must have overlooked it. I'm sorry. I know I am very careless, but nothing like this has ever happened before. I don't know what Sir Wilfred will say when he hears about this. The pearls were his gift on the anniversary of our silver wedding. Have you any clues, Inspector?"

"Not at the moment. I presume the servants are quite above suspicion?"

"I am sure they are all honest. Thomas, the butler, has been with us for seventeen years, and none of the three maids less than six years. I am notoriously careless, and yet I have never missed anything. I will vouch for the servants."

"What was the value of the necklace?"

"I think about five thousand pounds."

"Insured?"

"No."

"Is there any person outside members of the household who knows you are in the habit of keeping your trinket box in the wardrobe?"

"Oh yes—but only intimate friends, who have

had occasion to be in my bedroom while I was dressing."

"Was it common knowledge that you and Sir Wilfred would be out of town last evening?"

"I may have told a few people at a bridge drive which I attended the previous day. I really forget."

McLean sighed in despair. Here was a woman who apparently notified her intention of going away for the night and leaving a five-thousand-pound necklace in an open drawer. It was scarcely fair on the thief.

On going down into the hall, with a view to making a closer examination of the outside of the house, he found a tall youngish man interrogating the butler. He had a large note-book in his hand and was writing shorthand furiously.

"What is your business?" inquired McLean.

"Local newspaper. I have only just heard the news. You don't mind me taking a few notes?"

"Not at all."

"Thanks awfully. Any clues?"

"Lots," replied McLean dryly. "But they are not for publication—yet."

"But the green feathers—can't I say anything about them?"

"Say what you like. If you have got a theory about them you are welcome to it."

"Thanks awfully. My name's Littlejohn."

McLean left him to get what details he could

from members of the household. He could understand the man's excitement and enthusiasm, for Sir Wilfred was a magistrate on the local bench, chairman of the hospital and sundry other things. While to a first-class London newspaper the robbery would be of decidedly second-rate importance, to the local paper it was a positive scoop.

The means of entry still puzzled McLean. There was no basement area to the house, and all the ground-floor windows were fitted with stout shutters. On the upper floor the windows were not shuttered, but they were particularly difficult of access from below, though not absolutely safe from a cat-burglar. But the house had recently been decorated on the outside, and the new paint was unscratched everywhere.

McLean was examining a very tall wireless mast with interest when Littlejohn left the house and crossed the lawn. He looked quite pleased with himself and whistled as he approached McLean. McLean simulated entire ignorance of his presence for a few moments.

" I say, Inspector ? "

" Well ? "

" I've got a theory."

" Really ! "

" You don't want to listen to it ? "

" Well, I am rather busy at the moment. Tell me some other time."

Littlejohn looked extremely hurt, and finally went away in disgust. Later McLean satisfied himself on one point—the method of entry. It was daring and spectacular. From the wireless mast to the window through which the aerial went was some seventy feet, but the corner of the house where Lady Dyson had her bedroom projected considerably and was very much nearer the mast. Some thirty feet to the rear of the mast was a towering elm tree, with a long limb twenty feet from the ground. An agile man could have swarmed up the tree with ease, and this had evidently been done, for there was evidence in the shape of scored bark and broken twigs. The other part of the operation lay with the wireless mast. It was necessary for the robber to scale that, and fasten a length of rope to the top of it. Using the elm branch as a platform, the intending house-breaker could swing through space and make a landing on the eaves of Lady Dyson's window. A kind of circus act, but not at all impossible in the circumstances.

A close examination of the wireless mast proved that this had been done. Moreover, it provided a valuable clue—a thread of cloth caught by a splinter—presumably in a rapid descent. Lady Dyson's window had been found unlatched, but whether or not she had left it in that condition was not established. Even if she had, the prising aside of the catch would not have been a difficult matter to a thief provided with a tool.

It was all that was achieved that day, and McLean went home to ponder the next move. The following morning he bought a copy of the local newspaper. As he fully expected, there was a very long account of the robbery. Mr. Littlejohn had done his job well. It read like a work of fiction, and was most graphically written. But what took McLean's breath away was the journalist's temerity in putting forward a theory. He had a dig at the police. They were obsessed with antiquated methods, and unwilling to consider suggestions. They were baffled by the scattering of feathers and by the initials found on the window-pane. Mr. Littlejohn (presumably) now begged to expound his theory. Two years ago a man had come before Sir Wilfred Dyson on a charge of housebreaking. The case was proved and the man was found to be a bad character. Sir Wilfred had sentenced him to twelve months' imprisonment with hard labour. Now, strangely enough, this man kept a small public-house in the neighbourhood called " The Feathers," and his name was Oliver Lashing. Were these coincidences of no importance? Did it not appear to be an act of revenge and spite? The paper was following the case carefully and would have more to say about it on the following day.

McLean threw the newspaper across to Sergeant Brook, who had been making inquiries in certain quarters with reference to the missing jewels. Brook read the long article and uttered a growl of resentment as he reached the end.

"Darned cheek! Who wrote this, Inspector?"

"A gentleman named Littlejohn, gifted with a rich imagination. Quite well done too."

"There's nothing in it, is there?"

"A coincidence, I imagine. However much spite this man may have had it is scarcely likely that he would reveal his identity to Sir Wilfred. Mr. Littlejohn apparently overlooked that natural flaw in his argument. On the other hand, he may not have cared. Journalists' and editors' jobs are to sell their paper. Sir Wilfred is due home to-day. I will mention the matter to him."

McLean found Sir Wilfred later in the morning. He had already read the article in the newspaper, and had formed an opinion quite different from what McLean expected.

"I remember the case clearly," he said. "Lashing was a brute of a fellow. His public-house was a blind, and he derived a livelihood from other sources—bookmaking, larcency, et cetera. He was an impudent rascal, incorrigible and fearless."

"But you do not think he was capable of robbing you, and leaving his initials on the window?"

"That is not unlikely. He might give himself

away by so acting, but he would be cunning enough to know that we cannot use those facts as evidence. Provided he can conceal his loot he is quite safe."

"What happened to him after his release from jail?"

"I don't know. The public-house changed hands, and he disappeared. It was smart of that Press man to recall the case."

McLean frowned, but made no further comment. As he was leaving the grounds Mr. Littlejohn turned up. He greeted McLean with a cheery smile.

"Hullo, Inspector! Seen the old paper?"

"I have had that pleasure. Congratulations!"

"You aren't sore about it?"

"Why should I be?"

"Well, I tried to tell you before I wrote it up, but you didn't seem very keen to listen."

"I misunderstood you."

"Well, it was just a bit of luck. You see, I couldn't help remembering about Lashing, and his connection with 'The Feathers.' I had to attend Court to report the case. Horrible fellow he was. Glared at the magistrate, and laughed mockingly when he was sentenced. As he left the dock I heard him say, 'You'll hear from me again, old bean!'"

"We have yet to prove that he has been heard from."

"I know. But you must admit the coincidence is a bit strong. What beats me is how he got into the house. But I'm going to find out."

"So that is why you are here?"

"Well, yes. This case is giving the paper quite a fillip. It's our own little private burglary, so to speak. If I discover anything really important I'll let you know."

"That is very kind of you."

Littlejohn went off in the direction of the wireless mast, and McLean wondered at his amazing conceit.

§

The article in the local newspaper did not pass unnoticed by the more important journals. There were quotations from it in several evening papers who seemed to take the theory seriously.

"We'll have to look up this fellow Lashing," said McLean to Brook. "See what you can find out at 'The Feathers.' The business was sold after Lashing's release from prison, and the present owner may know Lashing's address."

Brook's subsequent inquiries led him from London to Birmingham. In the latter city he discovered that Lashing had bought another public-house apparently with the proceeds from the sale of "The Feathers," but he had only run the place for six months, after which he sold out again and vanished.

"A dead end," said Brook. "But I've got photographs, taken recently. They don't agree with those in our records. He has since grown a moustache and wears his hair differently."

He produced the prints, and McLean compared them with those they already possessed. In two years Lashing had changed considerably, but there was no difficulty in recognising him.

"Try Rohmers and the 'White Knight,'" suggested McLean. "I'll look up some other places myself."

To keep the thing alive, out came the local newspaper with some new discoveries. One was an enormous footprint behind a rhododendron bush in Sir Wilfred's garden, and the other was a note found in the letter-box of the journal, and addressed to the editor in printed characters. It ran:

> "The police can do their own dirty work. You mind your own business, or you may be sorry.—O.L."

"This is about the limit," snarled Brook. "Why weren't we advised before they published this?"

McLean was not greatly perturbed. All he did was to notify his intention of seeing the footprint mentioned in the newspaper. He rang up Littlejohn and begged him to meet him at the house in an hour's time. Littlejohn kept the appointment.

"I am anxious to see the footprint," said McLean.

"I thought you would be. I telephoned you immediately I discovered it, but couldn't get on to you. We go to press early and I had to get on with my 'copy.'"

"Don't you know it is rather irregular to publish such details without the sanction of the police?"

"I didn't know that. Of course I promised to tell you, but how could I when you were not there?"

"You were thinking more about your paper?"

"Well, I have to consider it."

"Quite. We will say no more about it. Now, where is this footprint?"

"Near the wall yonder. The burglar must have feared to leave by the main gate, and walked down the path to the end of the garden. Near the rhododendron bush he left the path and made for the wall. Unfortunately his left foot fell on a muddy spot and left a clear impression. It was almost dark when I came across it."

He led McLean to the place indicated, and Lean found the impression. It was very clear and particularly large. The sole of the boot that made it was without nails, but the heel bore a covering of rubber. McLean took out a small pair of scissors and cut a piece of paper to the exact shape.

"Out-size," he mused. "At least a No. 10 boot."

"Yes. I measured it. It is over twelve inches long."

"Interesting. Lashing was six feet in height."

"Doesn't it all fit in with the theory?"

"I am inclined to admit it does. You ought to have been a detective, Mr. Littlejohn."

"Oh no. It was all luck on my part. I just wanted to get a good story. You see, a local burglary is more important than a distant murder with us. Our circulation is purely local, and everyone knows Sir Wilfred. If the burglar is ultimately caught it will be a splendid thing for the paper."

"It seems to be a splendid thing already. Did you bring that note along with you?"

"Note! Oh yes, the letter. Here it is."

McLean perused the note with its threat, but he made no comment, other than to ask if he might retain it, which he was permitted to do. When he saw Brook again the sergeant reported no progress. He had visited several haunts without discovering anything of importance. Lashing was known to certain crooks, but none of them had seen the man for some time—according to them.

"Did you see the footprint?" asked Brook.

"Oh yes."

"Then it wasn't an invention?"

"Not at all. It is as plain as the nose on one's face. There is only one remarkable fact about it."

Brook looked up questioningly.

"The remarkable fact is," resumed McLean, "that it was not there yesterday afternoon."

"Well, I'm——!"

"That part is a pure swindle to back up the theory. Littlejohn was stuck for a new instalment. He had made a splendid start, and wanted to go on. Of course he knew Lashing was a tall man, may even have noticed that he had feet of abnormal size."

"By Jove! That is sailing pretty close to the wind!"

"Very close. Shortly we may have to take steps to interrupt the continuation of his thrilling serial."

"But the letter?"

"A man who will fabricate footprints will also fabricate letters. This is journalism gone mad."

"But the editor——?"

"A sleepy old man with no sense of his responsibilities. Mr. Littlejohn aspires to be editor, contributor in chief, and detective at one shot. So far he has done very well."

"You believe in his theory?"

"No."

"But you want Lashing?"

"I do."

"Then there is some connection?"

"I think so."

§

Two days later Lashing was found. McLean had pulled many strings in vain, but at last he pulled the right one. He met an old " lag " who had seen Lashing a few days previously. Some money passed and McLean was given an address. Late in the evening Lashing came home to find McLean waiting for him. His thieves' instinct told him that this was a police officer.

" What do you want ? " he snarled.

" You are Oliver Lashing ? "

" That's my name. You're a nark I reckon ? "

" My name is McLean."

" I've heard of you. What do you want me for ? I'm going straight now."

" That would be rather remarkable—if it were true. I merely want you to answer a few questions, and I believe you will answer them to my satisfaction. You may have heard that Sir Wilfred Dyson's house was entered on March the tenth, and some valuable jewellery taken ? "

" I have, and I've seen the damned lies the papers are printing—hinting it might be me. If I had money enough I'd make them pay. It's plain libel."

" Well, where were you on that night ? "

" In York. I've got a bill here from a hotel, and

witnesses to prove that I was actually there at eleven o'clock at night, and six o'clock the next morning, when I had a cup of tea brought to my room. If you think I handled that job——"

"I am inclined to think you did not. But you may know who did?"

"I don't. I'm out of that business now. Sticking to the 'gees' and doing well."

"Did you ever know a man named Briscoe?"

Lashing laughed amusedly.

"I should say I did. Cleverest chap in our business—I mean the old business. And no one would ever think so to look at him. In strict confidence I done a few jobs with him. Agile as a blooming cat. Did a bunk to Australia two years ago, and died there I heard later."

"What sort of a man was he?"

"Well educated. Had a public-school education —so he used to boast. The cops never got any change out of Ned Briscoe. He'd freeze on to the stuff under their very noses, and they knew he had it, but couldn't find it."

"What was the secret?"

"You'd never guess. He used to be on the halls doing swallowing stunts. That man could swallow anything up to a full-size watch, and disgorge it when he wanted to. Most uncanny he was."

"And now he is dead?"

"Yes. Run over by a car in Sydney—so I heard."

"You'd know his photograph if you saw it?"

"You bet I would."

"Then take a glance at that."

McLean produced a small print and handed it to Lashing. As soon as he saw it he nodded his head.

"That's him—but he used to wear a moustache—kind of Charlie Chaplin thing. Looks innocent enough, don't he?"

"Quite."

It was all McLean required of Lashing. Half an hour later he was with Brook.

"I've found Oliver Lashing," said McLean. "The poor man has been badly libelled."

"So it wasn't he?"

"Oh no. I never thought it was for a moment, but I was anxious to see him for a particular reason. I thought he might happen to know a Mr. Briscoe."

"Briscoe! Not Ned Briscoe?"

"The same. You knew him?"

"Only as a name. There were lots of charges against him, but not one of them could be proved. He disappeared suddenly."

"Well, now we are going to resurrect him. As a matter of fact I have already been to his lodgings —while he was not there—and I have every reason to believe it was Briscoe who did the Dyson job."

" Then the theory about the feathers and the initials was all wrong ? "

" A plan on the part of the burglar to make it look as if our old friend Lashing was culpable. He and Lashing used to work together."

" By Jove, then Littlejohn was somewhere near the truth ? "

McLean smiled, and told Brook he required him at once to make an arrest.

" Briscoe ? "

" Yes. I know where I can put my hands on him."

They went out together, and took a taxi northwards. Half an hour later they alighted outside a big apartment house. On the first floor McLean stopped before a door which to Brook's amazement bore the card of Mr. Littlejohn.

" The journalist," he gasped. " You don't mean he is Ned Briscoe ? "

" I do. He made a big *faux pas*. He stated that he was present at the trial of Lashing. But upon making a few inquiries about him I discovered that he had been on the staff of the newspaper for one year only. He went to Australia, did some journalistic work there, and then came back under the name of Littlejohn, and decided to pose as a respectable journalist. Fortunately I discovered an old envelope bearing the name of Briscoe."

" And the stuff—the booty ? "

"I think we shall get that all right."

McLean thereupon pushed the bell button, and a small maid appeared. Instead of going straight in, McLean told the girl to tell her employer that Inspector McLean wished to see him at once.

"That will give him time," muttered Brook.

"Precisely. I want him to have a little time. It will save a lot of searching in the long run."

Two minutes later the girl came back and said that Mr. Littlejohn would be pleased to see Inspector McLean. They passed through a hall and into a sitting-room where Littlejohn was busy writing. He smiled and welcomed his visitors.

"Just finished," he said. "Got to get this to press within half an hour. I prefer to work at home."

"More theories?" asked McLean.

"Oh no. We have dropped the Dyson case. Can't run a stunt for ever."

"I met an old friend of yours to-day," said McLean. "A Mr. Oliver Lashing."

Littlejohn gazed at him incredulously.

"You—you have arrested him?" he asked.

"Oh no. He had nothing to do with it."

"But the feathers and the initials?"

"They were very cleverly arranged by an old friend of Lashing's—a Mr. Ned Briscoe. That, in short, is the object of my visit—to arrest you, Mr. Briscoe, on a charge of larceny."

The journalist stood up, and then laughed.

"Is this a joke?"

"Oh no. When you scaled the wireless mast you left a piece of thread on a splinter. The coat it came from is in that cupboard, also the feather duster from which you removed a supply of feathers. The boot you used to make the imprint is not on the premises, but that is not vitally important."

Briscoe seemed to realise that he was in a tight corner, but he still blustered.

"You dare to suggest that I have Lady Dyson's jewels?" he asked.

"I do, and I should advise you to produce them at once."

"You are terribly mistaken. The place is at your disposal. Find the jewels."

McLean stepped forward and tapped him on the chest.

"I'll give you two minutes to produce the necklace and the rings. In your own interest I advise you to hand them over."

"I tell you I have not got them. I have never seen them."

"Then we must use an emetic—but not here. Get him, Brook! We have wasted enough time."

"An emet——!" gasped Briscoe.

"After the X-rays, of course. Nasty things emetics—when they are made particularly strong!"

"Wait!" cried Briscoe. "I'm through. Another twelve hours and I would have given you a fine run. Lashing must have told you—the rat!"

"He believed you were dead. Hurry up!"

Briscoe turned his head slightly, made a few convulsive movements, and finally deposited the missing jewellery into Brook's large handkerchief.

"The first time it has let me down," he said bitterly.

"Where is the trinket box?"

"I burnt it. Do I look the sort of fool who would let a thing like that hang about? I kept the stuff in my pocket to swallow at any moment. I've got a man in South Africa waiting for the pearls. Let me have a drink before I go. This swallowing business gives me a devil of a thirst."

He helped himself to a huge whisky-and-soda, and then became cheerful.

"Exit Mr. Littlejohn!" he said. "Well, it was a rotten name."

XIV

§

It was on a wild and snowy morning in December that Scotland Yard received the news of the Tausig robbery, and McLean was sent along to investigate the matter. Sir Julius Tausig was well known in London society as a generous benefactor to numerous charities, and an influential member of the Stock Exchange. His wealth was reputed to be fabulous, and in addition he was a man of charming personality.

His house in Regent's Park was one of a row of six terrace dwellings, not very imposing in itself, but richly furnished, and packed with valuable art treasures. Years ago it had come to the notice of the police that Sir Julius was marked down by a certain gang of thieves, but no attempt had been made until now. In the meantime Sir Julius had taken every precaution possible, to safeguard his property, and some of his devices were most ingenious.

McLean found the millionaire pacing his library in a state of bewilderment. The north side of the room was in a shocking state, for an aperture nearly two feet square had been made through the wall, and plaster and bits of wall-paper were strewn about the floor.

"Inspector McLean?"

"Yes, Sir Julius. This appears to be a bit daring."

"Amazing. As you can see, entry was made from the next house—through a two-feet wall. Of course the place is empty now."

"Naturally. I should be glad of the details."

"My butler discovered the robbery this morning. The most astonishing thing is that none of us was disturbed during the night. I dined out and arrived home shortly after midnight. Lady Tausig is out of town. The staff comprised my butler and three maids."

"What does your loss consist of?"

"Practically nothing. The safe was opened by some ingenious instrument and a sum of fifty pounds in notes was taken, also a sheet of old Victorian postage stamps which I kept in the cash-box."

"Were the stamps of any great value?"

"I have been told they were worth a hundred pounds."

"I should like to see the safe."

It formed part of the wall on the west side of the room. A push-button operated the outer door, which was camouflaged by some moulding. When the steel door came to view, McLean saw that an oxy-acetylene apparatus had been used. The steel had run like butter. It was clear that the thing was the work of very experienced men.

"You found the safe door open?"

"No—closed. When I entered the room, the only disturbance was the breach in the wall."

"And your vanished neighbour?"

"The next-door house belongs to a Mrs. Beeching—a wealthy and highly respected widow, now staying at Mentone for the winter. She let her house in October—furnished. I never saw any of the tenants, but my butler tells me he has seen two men and a young woman. They apparently brought their own servants."

McLean stepped through the breach in the wall and found himself in a kind of study. After spending a few minutes there he explored the neighbouring house. As he expected, there was nothing there to give him a clue to the late occupants. He came back.

"A clean escape. We must interrogate the agent, but I doubt if we shall learn much. I am afraid you have been the victim of an exceedingly clever gang. The thing was evidently planned from the time of occupation, and the wall pierced little by little, until the moment was ripe to break through the last thin section. But I understood you had taken every precaution against burglars?"

"That is the amazing thing about it. I had the room specially wired so that any intrusion would ring a loud alarm upstairs. All the windows, as you can see, face the street, and have stout shutters. In addition I had a special powerful white light concealed in the pendant. The floor is slightly sprung all round, and when the switch is set, that light comes on immediately any person sets foot on the floor."

"With what object, if the windows are shuttered?"

"I will show you. It is a device of my own invention, and carried out by a firm of opticians."

He went to the wall almost immediately opposite the safe, and on pressing a button revealed a deep recess. In the recess was a camera, with its comparatively small lens pointing through a hole. McLean saw a spool and some clockwork mechanism.

"Cinematographic?"

"Yes. The white light is sufficiently powerful for the sensitive film used. When the light comes on it sets the camera working, and about fifty feet of film is exposed. The lens is of such angle as to take in everything that happens in the room beyond a radius of six feet."

"And did it work?"

"Yes. I took the film out this morning and sent it at once to be developed. I am promised prints within two hours."

"That is interesting. The bell alarm did not work?"

"No. It was put out of action. They must have discovered its existence."

There were several points which puzzled McLean. The robbers must have gone to great expense in order to carry out their scheme, and yet their plunder was worth, according to Sir Julius, no more than a hundred and fifty pounds.

"Are you sure about the stamps?" he inquired. "Is it possible you are mistaken about their real value?"

"Not to any extent. They might be worth two hundred pounds at the most—certainly not more. I retained them out of sentiment, for they were found in an old bureau belonging to my father. It is true I have certain jewellery in the house, but it is not kept in this room, and I have assured myself it is safe."

"Then the thieves have got a bad bargain?"

"It looks very much like it."

"Yet they knew of the existence of the bell alarm? No, there is something we don't understand at the moment. Men who go to all this trouble usually know what they are after and where it can be found. They have been watching you for three months—probably through a minute peephole in the wall. You had better make sure that all your treasures are safe."

"I will do that immediately, but I feel sure the thieves did not leave this room, in which case only the money and stamps are missing."

"The cinematographic prints may tell us something."

"I hope so."

McLean saw the butler and the other servants for a few moments, but they had nothing new to tell him. From Sir Julius he got the address of the agent who had let the house next door. Pending the arrival of the cinematographic prints McLean interviewed the agent. The man was amazed when he heard what had happened.

"But they were the nicest people," he protested.

"Whom did you see in reference to the letting?"

"A Colonel Dingle and his wife."

"Did they furnish references?"

"There was no need. The Colonel made no demur when I asked for the rent in advance."

"Did he give you a cheque?"

"No—cash. Three hundred guineas for the three months."

"Wasn't that rather unusual?"

"Well, yes. But he explained that he had only just come home from India and was in process of changing his banking account."

"Can you describe these people?"

"Not in detail. I see so many clients. But I recall that the Colonel was fairly tall, and had grey hair and a grey moustache. His wife seemed much younger—probably forty. A dark woman and quite pretty."

The information gleaned in that direction was not of great value. On being pressed the agent became confused. It was evident he had no very clear recollection of his clients. McLean spent half an hour in his office and then returned to the scene of the robbery. The prints had arrived, and McLean took them eagerly. Of the fifty feet of film which had been exposed, only three feet contained photographs. On examining these the reason was clear. They revealed three figures— two men and a woman—chiefly back views. But at the end of the series one of the men had turned round. His face was in absolute focus, and his eyes raised apparently towards the source of illumination. The last few pictures showed him standing on a chair, removing the electric lamp. After that came blanks.

"Did you find the lamp in its socket?" inquired McLean.

"Yes."

"Then he must have replaced it. There is no doubt he feared the bright light would penetrate the shutters, and removed it quickly. But he did not suspect the camera."

"That is feasible," replied Sir Julius. "For the camera works absolutely silently. Do you know that man?"

McLean scanned the face, with its surprised expression, its strong and very prominent teeth and slight, scrubby moustache. At the moment he could not recall any notorious safe-cracker who bore any close resemblance to the man. His companions—presumably the Colonel and his wife—were not seen full-face, and it was doubtful whether their photographs could be used for purposes of identification.

"I don't know him," he said. "But the film is of the utmost value. I shall need to retain it."

"Certainly."

"Have you had time to take an inventory of your belongings?"

"Yes. There is nothing missing save the money and the stamps. The whole thing was a comparative failure."

McLean shook his head doubtfully. But for the overlooking of the camera a perfect job had been done. It seemed to him certain that the thieves would have taken many things that were left untouched had they failed to get what they really came for. Again he went into the neighbouring house and made another long investigation. It was in the kitchen—of all unlikely places—that he made a small discovery. On the floor were four common flat-headed tacks. He picked them up and found that three of them were bent.

The discovery in itself seemed trivial, but the kitchen bore every sign of having been thoroughly cleaned up quite recently. Obviously the tacks had been extracted from something. They led him to a new line of thought, and a little later he went and found Sir Julius.

" A clue, Inspector ? "

" A possible clue to the motive. Will you come into the library for a few moments ? I want to assure myself on a certain point."

The long room contained many paintings, hanging on the line of sight. They varied in size from quite small etchings to large oil-paintings.

" Some of these are doubtless valuable ? "

" Oh, yes, practically all of them. But two are masterpieces—the Rembrandt and the Gainsborough—there."

" They are—all right ? "

" Why, of course."

" Have you looked closely ? "

Sir Julius wrinkled his brow, and walked up to the Gainsborough. It was a beautiful piece of work, and he was perfectly satisfied that it had not been tampered with, but when he reached the Rembrandt he uttered a gasp.

"Well?"

"It's—it isn't the same! There's a difference. Great Heavens—I believe——"

McLean passed him and took the picture down. On turning it over he saw that the canvas was attached to the old frame by a number of new tacks in company with a few of different type.

"A substitute!" gasped Sir Julius.

"You are sure?"

"Positive—now. This is but a copy—one of the many that are in existence. That picture was worth fifty thousand pounds."

§

So the Tausig robbery, instead of being a matter of minor importance, now figured as one of the most daring exploits of recent times. The Press made a fine story out of it. The famous picture was reproduced in newspapers from John o' Groats to Land's End, and a big reward was offered by Sir Julius for the recovery of the masterpiece.

But the business of the cinematographic film remained the secret of the police and of Sir Julius. McLean now found his hands fairly full, for many different avenues had to be explored. Already he had a fairly long list of possible culprits—men who were known to engage in " big business," and who were capable of carrying out such a coup as this.

" You saw Sharkey ? " he inquired of Sergeant Brook.

" Yes. He knows nothing. I can prove that Sharkey was in Birmingham that night. I didn't think we should have any luck there. More like a MacMahon job."

" MacMahon is in jail. But I intend seeing him."

This McLean did the same afternoon. MacMahon had to his credit as many crimes as he had years to his age, and he had only been convicted once, and then on a minor charge. He was of a philosophical nature and looked upon life as a huge gamble. For the police he had an almost brotherly affection, and he welcomed McLean quite warmly.

" What's the latest scandal ? " he inquired.

" I want your help."

" Splendid. Who's been kicking you ? "

" Here's a photograph. Have a look at it."

MacMahon took the small print which McLean produced and scanned it with his keen eyes. It showed the three figures, the one full-faced and the others quarter-face—and rather vague.

" Don't know the fellow with the teeth," he mused. " But the tall chap seems a bit familiar. Haven't you got an enlargement ? "

"Yes. But I don't think it helps. Here it is."

The convict pursed his lips as he gazed at the larger print. He turned to the smaller print again.

"Cinematograph—eh?"

"Yes."

"Any more of it?"

"Yes—three feet."

"Couldn't you fire it off? I'd be able to tell you for certain then. If it's the fellow I think it is I'll tell you all I know about him. The dirty dog once played a low trick on me."

McLean promised to put the film through a projector, and two hours later this was done. MacMahon nodded his head when he saw the result.

"That's him—Fenlake. He's got a limp—see! He can hide that up when he likes, but he always limps when he's alone, or with pals. I don't know the woman nor the other man, but I'll swear that is Fenlake. You can find him at Shepherd's Bush—Conroy Mansions. And if you do get him, you can tell him I told you—and to hell with him!"

That night McLean and Brook visited Conroy Mansions. There was no man living there of the name of Fenlake, but upon his mentioning a tall man with a slight limp, McLean was informed that a Mr. Riley answered that description. He had a flat on the third floor, but was out at the moment. Possessing the necessary authority, McLean and Brook entered the flat. A search revealed nothing incriminating, but by the telephone there was a list of names and numbers, and added to this—in pencil—was the letter Q with a number. McLean had just made a note of this when the occupier of the apartment returned. As he entered the door McLean noticed the limp, but immediately it vanished. The hair was not the hair of Colonel Dingle, but dark and luxuriant. He faced the two intruders angrily.

"What is the meaning of this?" he demanded.

"We are police officers with a search warrant," said McLean. "I am under the impression that your name is Fenlake, alias Colonel Dingle."

"You are grossly misinformed."

"I regret I shall have to detain you pending further inquiries."

"This is infamous."

"In the meantime I should like to make a telephone call."

He went to the instrument, and called up the number appended to the letter Q. Fenlake gave a start as the numerals were given, and it did not escape McLean's hawk-like eyes. A few seconds later a woman's voice was heard. McLean gave a fine imitation of Fenlake's rasping voice.

"Is that you? Fenlake speaking. Something unexpected has happened. It is necessary for me to see you at once. Come to my flat immediately. I can't explain on the 'phone."

"All right, I'll be with you in ten minutes."

McLean hung up the receiver. Fenlake relapsed into a sullen silence.

"It would be rather remarkable if that young woman should come here," he mused. "Seeing that your name is not Fenlake."

"What if it is?"

"Why conceal it?"

"There is nothing criminal in that."

"Perhaps not. But I rather fancy our caller will turn out to be Mrs. Colonel Dingle. We shall see."

About a quarter of an hour later there was a ring at the bell. Brook was sent to the door, and admitted a well-built woman of about forty years of age. She was not the dark beauty mentioned by the house agent, but fair and blonde, and she stood bewildered when she saw Fenlake with his two visitors. Fenlake was about to blurt out something, but McLean prevented him.

"Ah, Mrs. Dingle," said McLean.

"I don't understand you. My name is Hunter."

"You are a friend of Mr. Fenlake?"

"Yes. But who are you?"

"Inspector McLean. You know my business. Hadn't you better make a clean breast of everything?"

"I haven't an idea what you are talking about. My friend telephoned me on a matter of business, and——"

"It was I who telephoned you. On the twenty-third of September you and this man posed as Colonel and Mrs. Dingle and rented a house in Regent's Park. With the assistance of a third party you removed a valuable work of art——"

"Nonsense!"

"I want the name of the third party."

"You are making a tremendous mistake. On the night of the robbery I was at a dance with my friend here——"

Fenlake bit his lip as he realised she had made a terrible *faux pas*. She shut up immediately.

"I must ask you to come with us," said McLean. "You will have an opportunity to prove an alibi later."

There was no doubt now that the two were the persons in the photograph, but the identity of the third person—and probably the ring-leader—was still a mystery. At the station McLean tried to get the woman to shed some light on the matter, but she still pleaded ignorance of the whole affair. Upon getting her address, McLean went to her flat. There he found a bank paying-in slip dated a few days after the robbery. The sum was £500, and he rejoiced to see it was entered in the "cheques" column.

The subsequent inquiry at the bank revealed the fact that the cheque was drawn on the account of Andrew Morrison. Andrew Morrison's account, on being investigated, showed two payments of the same date—one for £500 to Violet Hunter and another for £1000 to Hugh Fenlake.

"Now for Mr. Andrew Morrison!" said McLean.

§

It took three weeks to find that illusive personage. He moved from hotel to hotel with monotonous regularity, but at last Brook and McLean found him in Glasgow. They had waited in the vestibule of the comparatively small hotel for four hours when at last Morrison arrived in a Rolls Royce. McLean got a shock when he saw him, for he was not in the least like the man in the photograph.

"It—it can't be our man," said Brook.

"It must be. And yet—— Anyway, we will go up."

They went to Morrison's room and knocked on the door. A voice bade them enter, and they found Morrison lying on his bed. He blinked and sat up.

"I thought it was the chambermaid," he said. "May I ask the reason for this call?"

"We are police officers," said McLean. "There are one or two points we should like cleared up. You know a man named Hugh Fenlake?"

"Fenlake? Oh, yes."

"And a woman named Violet Hunter?"

"She is Fenlake's fiancée."

"Recently you paid them fairly large sums of money."

"That is so."

"For what purpose?"

"That is a distinctly private matter. I was indebted to them and wished to settle an old account."

"The money was for services rendered?"

"Certainly it was. They helped me out of a financial difficulty pending the recovery of some money."

"Have you ever heard of Colonel Dingle?"

"Never."

"Have you ever stayed at a house in Regent's Park?"

"No."

"I am going to search this room."

"By all means, but I fail to understand your motive."

McLean hunted in the wardrobe, the two large trunks, the chest of drawers, and finally the bed. Morrison sat and smoked the whole time in perfect calmness. When McLean had finished he sighed impatiently.

"What did you expect to find, Inspector?"

"Nothing," snapped McLean. "And I have found it."

Morrison laughed amusedly and wished them good-day. They went out exasperated and puzzled

"He can't be the man," said Brook.

"He is, but I've got to prove it. There is just one chance—the cat."

"It was taken into the garage."

"Stay here while I go down. He may suspect. Don't let him get away."

Brook waited on the landing. In his humble opinion they were on the wrong track. Morrison looked no more like the man in the photograph than he did himself, and he was inclined to believe the story about the cheques.

McLean found the big car in the garage with no one in attendance. He took out the cushions, and at last found what he wanted. It was a long roll, carefully tied up and hidden in a recess under the back seat. One look at the contents was sufficient. It was the stolen canvas! But he had not finished yet. There were pockets in the four doors of the vehicle, and in one of these he discovered a small box. He opened it and his eyes shone with joy. Two minutes later he was with Brook on the stairs. Brook saw the roll and gasped.

"You've got it?"

"Yes."

"Then there are four people in the swindle?"

"No—only three."

"But——"

A figure was coming down the stairs. It was Morrison, and as he turned the corner he saw McLean with the roll in his hand. He realised at once that the game was up, and made a wild leap to pass the two men. Brook put out his foot, and tripped Morrison neatly. He fell head foremost and his temple came into violent impact with the corner of a stair. He lay quite still.

"Out!" said Brook. "That saves a lot of trouble."

"Get him on to the landing."

Brook carried the inert form down the few remaining stairs and propped him in the corner.

"He'll come round in a minute or two. But he isn't the man in the photograph."

"Brook, you will have to attend evening classes," said McLean. "A knowledge of physiognomy is necessary for our profession. It needs but two small alterations to make our friend the man in the photograph—a small moustache, stuck on with gum, and something else, which I have just found."

He leaned over the limp form, did something with his hand for a few seconds and then stood aside and burst a bombshell on Brook. Morrison was now the living image of the photograph.

"False teeth!" ejaculated Brook.

"Yes. A man may disguise himself with paint and bits of hair, but there is nothing like a change of teeth to effect a real transformation. He kept that ugly set for emergencies. I think you may handcuff him now, for he is just about to wake up."

Morrison opened his eyes, glared at the two officers, and then saw his normal dentistry in McLean's hand. The fearsome projecting teeth expressed their owner's ignominy.

"Better get a taxi," said McLean.

"Curse you!" snarled Morrison. "Someone must have given me away."

"You are right," replied McLean. "But it wasn't a human being. Just a small piece of glass in front of a very sensitive film. You have a very accommodating dentist."

XV

§

McLEAN arrived at Baron's Place to find the owner of the large detached house in a state of great agitation. He had given his name on the telephone as Arthur Prettyman, and his complaint was that his safe had been robbed. McLean knew the type quite well—a rather hard business man, very conventional, very thorough, and also very intolerant.

"Ah, Inspector!" he gasped. "Thank heavens you have come. I am perplexed—bewildered."

"Robbery, I understand?"

"Yes—my safe—in this room. It is extraordinary—incredible! Never in my life——"

"One moment. Let us start at the beginning. Where is the safe?"

"There—in the corner—behind the second panel. The push-button is behind the adjacent picture."

"Please operate it."

Prettyman nodded and went to the picture. He slipped his hand behind it and the second panel slid back, revealing a large steel safe with a brass knob and two locks.

" Permit me ! "

McLean came forward and examined the exterior of the safe. It was free from scratches or damage of any kind.

" Not forced ? " he asked.

" No. That is the mystery. Shall I open it ? "

" Please."

He produced a bunch of keys and selected two of them. They fitted the respective locks and the door swung open. McLean examined the locks. They were of very modern type and were thief-proof except to the expert safe-cracker.

" What does your loss consist of ? "

" Two hundred pounds. To be exact, two hundred and six pounds."

" In notes ? "

" Yes. The cash was untouched."

" When did this take place ? "

" Between six o'clock last evening and nine o'clock this morning. I should explain that I have a manufacturing business in the country, and it is my custom to go there on Saturdays and pay the wages. As there is no bank near the works I draw the cash in London and lodge it in this safe for the night."

" But yesterday was Thursday—not Friday."

" I know. But it was my intention to go fishing to-day, and I drew the money yesterday to save a trip into the City. This morning I was telephoned by my fishing friend, postponing our trip until to-morrow, and I decided to run down to the works to-day and leave the cash with my manager. When I opened the safe it was gone."

"Who were in the house last evening—from six o'clock onwards?"

"My wife, my son and daughter, and two maids. I had dinner at seven-thirty and then went to spend the evening with a very old friend."

"You took your keys with you?"

"Yes."

"There are no duplicate keys to the safe?"

"None."

"The three members of your family were at home all the evening?"

"Yes."

"At what time did they retire?"

"Just after eleven, I believe——"

"Never mind. I will question them myself. I presume they know of your loss?"

"Yes."

"Who locked up the house?"

"My son—Neale—just before he retired, and when I came home at midnight I made sure that the doors and windows were securely fastened."

"Were they in the same state this morning?"

"The maid assures me they were."

"Then suspicion rests upon someone inside the house?"

"That is the baffling part. The two maids have been with me for over five years. In any case you have to remember that the safe was securely locked."

"I was thinking of the possibility of your keys having been duplicated at some time or other."

"They never leave my pocket."

"You are quite sure you did lock the safe after depositing the money there?"

"Absolutely! Besides, it was locked when I went to it this morning."

"Are the keys necessary for that?"

"One of them is. The other lock will operate by slamming the door."

He demonstrated this point, and McLean was a little puzzled. A skilled cracksman might have opened the safe and left no mark, but it did not seem likely that such a person would enter in the early hours of the evening—before the windows and doors were fastened. Only the petty thief worked in that manner—one who would snatch and run.

"The maid may have made a mistake about the window fastenings," said McLean. "If one was open it would solve the mystery. Failing that, the theft must have been undertaken by someone in the house—or by some person in collusion with someone in the house. I should like to see the two maids."

Both girls displayed some nervousness at being closely questioned, and the elder one stuck to her story. She had found the front door bolted and all the downstairs windows fastened on the inside. For anyone to have entered, a bedroom window must have been used, which was rather improbable as all the bedrooms were occupied save two, the windows of which were still latched.

McLean dismissed them after a few minutes, and looked round the room. The safe was placed very high, and required a fairly tall person to reach the handle. There was a long table in the centre, and various antique chairs scattered about. The whole length of one wall was fitted with bookshelves.

" This is your library, I presume ? "

" Yes. The lounge is next door."

" Is this room exactly as you found it this morning ? "

" Yes. I have been here ever since I discovered my loss. It has not even been dusted yet."

This fact was evident, for there were several newspapers lying about dated the day before, and a cigarette end in an ash-tray. McLean picked up the latter.

" Yours ? " he asked.

" No. I do not smoke cigarettes. It must have been left by my son Neale."

" He is in the house at the moment ? "

" No. He is in business in the City and had to leave half an hour ago."

" Your daughter and wife are here ? "

" Yes—in the lounge. Would you care to see them ? "

"Yes. I should like to know whether they used this room to any extent last evening."

Mrs. Prettyman and her daughter were called in. The wife was a charming little woman of about fifty, and the daughter was very much like her mother. Both appeared to be perturbed at what had taken place the night before.

"This is Inspector McLean," said Prettyman. "He would like to put a few questions."

"I won't detain you long," said McLean. "I am trying to fix the time of the robbery. Did either of you have occasion to come into this room after dinner last night?"

"Yes," said Mrs. Prettyman. "I came in about nine o'clock to get a book to read. I don't think Ethel came in—did you, dear?"

The girl shook her head.

"Were the windows closed then?"

"I think so. I am sure I should have noticed them had they been open."

"You did not stay long?"

"Not more than five minutes. I chose a book and went back into the lounge. Ethel and Neale were playing about with the wireless set."

"At what time did you retire?"

"At half-past ten—my daughter and I. Neale sat on for a bit. I heard him come upstairs about half an hour later."

"He locked up?"

"Yes. He always does when my husband is not at home."

No information of any great importance was obtained, and they seemed to be relieved when he thanked them and permitted them to leave. Prettyman went out for a few minutes to answer a call on the telephone, and McLean's attention was taken by a beautiful antique footstool. It did not seem to harmonise with the rest of the furniture, and was obviously out of place there. Lying on a chair close to it was a newspaper—folded up. He turned the newspaper over, and found upon it a very faint impression of a foot. It was incomplete—showing but half a sole and a portion of heel, and there was a small brown stain upon the heel. He slipped the whole thing into his pocket as Prettyman returned.

"May I look over the rest of the house?" he inquired.

"Certainly. Shall I accompany——?"

"It doesn't matter. I shall not be long."

He spent a quarter of an hour prowling about, and at length he found what he wanted—a piece of floor that had been recently stained and was still a trifle "tacky." It lay between three bedroom doors. Before he left he inquired who occupied the rooms, and was informed that they belonged to Mrs. Prettyman, her daughter and son respectively.

"I am going to the bank," he said finally. "It may be possible to get the numbers of some of the notes. I will call again this evening, in case your son may be able to help."

"I doubt it very much," said Prettyman. "But come by all means. Here is the address of the bank."

§

McLean's subsequent visit to the bank was fruitful. The stolen money included ten five-pound notes, the numbers of which had been noted by the cashier. This simplified matters considerably and McLean issued the necessary precautions. That evening he called again on Prettyman.

"I have the numbers of some of the notes," he said. "But I should like you not to divulge that fact to anyone."

Prettyman looked at him sharply.

"It is evident you think the thief is in this house?"

"It is possible. May I now see your son?"

Neale Prettyman was shown into the library. He was a well-built man of twenty-six, and perfectly at his ease. McLean asked him a lot of questions, all of which were answered without pause. He admitted he had known the money was in the safe, and on that account he took great care to assure himself that the house was locked up before he went to bed.

"The maids had retired then?"

"Yes. Only my father was up, and he told us

he did not expect to return until about midnight. I put out all the lights except the one in the hall. My father, of course, had his latch-key."

McLean found himself unusually interested in the case, comparatively trivial as it was. He believed that the two maids were quite innocent of collusion with any outside person, and so far as could be gathered neither of them knew that the safe contained any considerable sum of money. On the other hand, it was equally improbable that the house had been entered. The clue of the footprint puzzled him. Evidently a person of small stature had stood upon the stool in order to reach the safe, and the same person had not long previously stepped on to the newly-stained section of floor. The natural deduction was that the thief was a woman, but he was loath to jump to hasty conclusions. The obvious thing to do was to find the shoe or slipper that had made the impression.

This he failed to do, and he was obliged to postpone his investigations for the present. Several days passed, and then one of the missing notes was traced. It had been paid into the bank by a tradesman in the neighbourhood, and upon being questioned the man stated positively that the note was given him by Ethel Prettyman, who had purchased a wrist watch on the twentieth—two days after the robbery!

McLean made it his business to see the girl, and chose a time when Prettyman was not at home.

The first thing he saw was the new wrist-watch. She could not but notice his long glance at the object, and was evidently puzzled by his interest in it.

"I think you were not wearing that watch when I saw you before, Miss Prettyman?" he asked.

"No. I broke my old one months ago. I have only had this one three days. But why——?"

"A present perhaps?"

"Yes. The nineteenth was my birthday."

"Your father's gift?"

"No. Why do you ask me such questions?"

"A matter of some importance is involved. Am I right in believing that you bought that watch yourself?"

"Yes."

"With your own money?"

"Certainly." She flushed up at the innuendo. "What are you trying to suggest?"

"Nothing at the moment, but I should be grateful if you would explain how you came to be in possession of the five-pound note which you paid to the jeweller?"

"My brother gave it to me. He wanted to buy me something for my birthday, and did not know what to get. To solve the difficulty he left me an envelope with the note inside it, and asked me to buy something that I needed."

"Ah! I never thought of that. You must forgive my curiosity."

He was about to go, but she caught his arm and looked at him anxiously.

"You—you are hiding something? It is in connection with that robbery. You—you can't possibly imagine that my brother—my own brother—— It is absurd!"

"I am not making any accusations."

"But——!"

"That is all I can say. I am sorry to have troubled you."

Ethel's admission gave McLean seriously to think. In the library he had found the stump of a cigarette which Prettyman had stated was left there by his son. The stained portion of floor was adjacent to Neale's room, and now this note——! But the impression made on the newspaper seemed to be smaller than a man of Neale's stature would have left. Was the theory of the stool wrong? It certainly looked like it in the face of this new evidence.

Instead of waiting for Neale to come home, McLean interviewed him at his office. He was sales manager in a prosperous motor business, and when McLean was shown in, Neale was dictating letters to his secretary.

"I should like to see you alone, Mr. Prettyman."

"Certainly. Miss Jones, I will ring when I require you."

The girl vanished and Neale gazed at his visitor

inquiringly. It was evident he was puzzled by the visit.

"It is in connection with your sister's birthday," said McLean. "I understand you gave her a certain present?"

"Well, yes, but I don't understand what that——"

"Where did you get that note?"

Neale's mouth tightened. He was about to say something, when a look of alarm entered his eyes and he remained dumb.

"Hadn't you better tell me?"

"I—I can't remember. I cashed a cheque—somewhere, but at the moment——"

"Five-pound notes are not so common as all that. It happened to be a new one. Won't you reflect a little?"

Neale began to pace the room in a state of great agitation. At last he halted and faced McLean with his jaw thrust out pugnaciously.

"I can't remember, and that's the end of it."

"But it may not be the end of it. You will have guessed my reason for making this inquiry?"

"I think I know. You think—you imagine that I—I robbed my father's safe?"

"I am asking you to explain how you came to be in possession of one of the missing notes."

"It was passed on to me."

"By whom?"

"There I cannot help you."

"You put me in a difficult position, Mr. Prettyman."

"That means—I may be arrested?"

"Why not tell the truth?"

"You don't believe me when I tell you that I cannot remember where I got that note?"

"I do not. But I will give you twelve hours to reflect on the matter. After that——"

There was a knock on the door, and a clerk entered to inform Neale that his father had called and wished to see him. He looked at McLean.

"Ask him in," said McLean grimly.

"Very well."

Prettyman entered the room in a state of excitement. He started when he saw McLean, and gazed from the Inspector to his son's rather drawn countenance.

"I didn't expect to see you, Inspector," he said. "As a matter of fact I have been trying to get you on the telephone. I am afraid I have been guilty of gross carelessness. I—I have found the missing money."

"Found the——!"

"I had occasion to search for a document in the safe this afternoon. I found the notes behind the cash-box. I cannot imagine how they got there, but I recall that I was in rather a hurry when I put them into the safe. It is a great relief, and I must ask you to accept my deepest apologies for putting you to so much trouble."

McLean's brow came down. He saw Neale staring at his father incredulously.

"I am glad you have found them," he said ultimately. "No wonder we were baffled."

He went out and left the two men together.

§

Two hours later there occurred an incident which had a very close and unexpected connection with the Prettyman enigma. A man known to the police as a bad character was arrested for a crime committed a week before. His name was Lessing, and he had served many sentences during his adventurous life. Upon being searched a considerable sum of money was found on his person, and among this were four five-pound notes. Upon investigation these notes proved to be a portion of the missing batch. McLean's eyes gleamed when this information reached him. He went at once to the prisoner.

"Your name is Lessing?"

"Yes."

"These notes were found in your possession. Where did you get them?"

"That is my business."

"You may find it a very serious business. I am able to prove that these notes were stolen from a house in Baron's Place——"

"It's a lie!"

" You will have some difficulty in proving your innocence. We have you on one charge. The second charge will get you a further two years."

" I tell you——"

" That you got them honestly ? "

" Yes. They were given to me—by a friend."

" Someone named Prettyman ? "

Lessing hesitated and then inclined his head.

" I'll tell you the truth," he added. " They were given to me by my sister—Mrs. Prettyman. I was in a tight corner. After I came out of quod last September I managed to get a decent job. I meant to go straight, but things went all wrong. I did a bit of gambling and had to lay hands on the firm's money. Last week I realised that unless I made my accounts square, the accountants would discover the defalcations. I knew where my sister was living, though I had not seen her for many years. She was my only chance. I went to her and told her that unless I could raise two hundred pounds that night I would be arrested in the morning. She said she had not got that amount of money, but would go to her brother on the following day. I couldn't wait. I begged her to save me from imprisonment, and at last she consented. She asked me to wait, and then went out of the room. Ten minutes later she came back and handed me the money."

" What time was this ? "

" Just after seven o'clock in the evening."

"Did the maid let you into the house?"

"No. I saw my sister from the garden, and she let me into the drawing-room through the casement window."

"And you did not make good the defalcations?"

"No. I—I couldn't give up good money. I—I ran off with it, and went horse-racing. What there is left belongs to my sister. She had better have it. That's the whole truth."

It evidently was—so far as Lessing was concerned; but McLean was anxious to clear up one or two points. He called at Baron's Place, and after waiting an hour for Mrs. Prettyman to return from a shopping expedition, he saw her.

"Inspector," she gasped. "Did you wish to see my husband?"

"No, you yourself, madam. Yesterday we arrested a man named Lessing——"

"Lessing!" Her face went pallid.

"He had upon his person a considerable sum of money, which he stated belonged to you. I have brought it with me—one hundred and forty-two pounds in all. Curiously enough, these five-pound notes bear numbers which coincide with some of the notes which were missing—for a time. The cashier at the bank must have made a mistake, since Mr. Prettyman has recovered his money?"

She gulped and then hung her head.

"There was no mistake," she said. "These are the notes that were taken. I—I was the culprit.

There was no intention of theft. I had to find the money——"

" I know that part of the story."

" He—he told you ? "

" Yes. But what you do not know is that one of the missing notes was traced to your daughter, who got it from your son."

" My son ! Oh, I remember. It was afterwards. My son came to me and told me he wanted to give Ethel a present, but had not had time to buy anything—didn't know what to buy, in fact. He struck the idea of giving her a five-pound note, but possessed only smaller change. I had drawn some money from my own account that day and had two five-pound notes in my purse. I exchanged one with him."

" You evidently gave him one of the sto—one of those which came from the safe."

" Yes. I was agitated—worried by what I had done. When I opened the safe I took all the notes there were in it and put them into my purse. My—my brother demanded two hundred pounds. I gave him that amount—and he went away. That left me with several notes."

" How did you open the safe ? "

" My husband was in the bathroom, and his clothes were in the bedroom. I took his keys and replaced them later."

" And you used the footstool in order to reach the safe, and in your regard for its excellent upholstery you placed a sheet of newspaper over it ? "

" Yes, but how—— ? "

" When you went upstairs you trod upon some staining that was not quite dry. Ultimately you replaced the money in the safe ? "

" Yes. That was always my intention. I did not know that my husband had changed his mind and was going down to his works on the Friday instead of the Saturday. I bargained upon borrowing sufficient money from my brother to make my banking account good for two hundred pounds, and so make good the money in the safe. That—that is all there is to say."

McLean nodded, and was full of sympathy for her.

" Don't you think it would have been wiser to have told your husband the truth ? "

" Yes, but it all happened so suddenly. I was given no time to think. Depraved and dishonest as my brother is, I felt I ought to help him. My husband does not even know of his existence. I was ashamed—I dared not tell him that I was related to a habitual criminal. You—you do understand ? "

" I think I do," replied McLean. " Well, that is the end of the business. There is no need for him to be told—now."

She smiled and shook her head.

" There is every need. It is the only secret I

have ever hidden from him. To-night I shall tell him the truth, and trust I shall be forgiven."

"I am positive you will. I am afraid your brother will be put away again. He made light of your sacrifice by abusing your generosity. In future I should try to forget him."

"I mean to," she said determinedly. "Did—did my son tell you where he got the note?"

"Your son was ready to go to prison if need be."

"Ah!" she sighed, and her eyes grew glad.

McLean went back to the office, whistling to himself. It was good to have an occasional relief from the more brutal kind of case.

McLEAN INVESTIGATES   XVI

§

FOR months the Feeny gang had been after the Rajah's ruby, and at last their plan was close to maturity. On this evening in January a group of four men met at Feeny's flat and discussed all the details. Feeny was an Irish-American, and a notorious jewel thief whom the police had not yet succeeded in getting. All his schemes were planned with meticulous care, and he himself never touched a stolen article until it was thousands of miles away from its owner. Feeny was content to plan the scheme of campaign, and to let his skilled hirelings carry it out.

He was a bit of a dude in appearance—well-dressed, well-groomed, well-spoken, with a pretty wit when it suited him. But in an emergency he could prove desperate enough. His accomplices were a mixed trio—two men and a woman. One of the men was of the lower crook type, but the other was an educated man who had made a muck of his life and fallen into Feeny's hands. He, like Feeny, dressed well, and could pass as a gentleman anywhere. His name was Streeter—and once he had been a fine athlete. The rough man, with the bullet head, was Pat Dugan, and the woman was known as Dolly.

" You fixed things with Walters ? " asked Feeny, helping himself to a large glass of whisky.

Streeter nodded.

" Did you pay him ? "

" Only what you said—half the amount. I told him he would get the other fifty after the show."

" He knows his part ? "

" Perfectly well. He won't plead illness until about two hours before the reception. There is no other servant capable of being wine-steward, and Walters will recommend his brother—in other words, myself."

" And the electric wiring ? "

" I've got the whole lay-out. Pat can cut the main cable where it enters the house—during dinner, at a time when I am near the Rajah. He can see into the room through the window."

" Suppose the blinds are drawn ? "

"That blind will not be drawn. I shall put it out of order beforehand. The car will be in the road outside—away from the main parking place. Pat will go straight for the car, and I shall join him when I've got the ruby and change in the car. I can get rid of my servant's clothes *en route*—over a convenient hedge."

Feeny nodded his head and reflected for a moment.

"You've got to remember that there is a possibility of detectives being present. That devil McLean prevented the last attempt."

"I know. I shall slip the ruby into my mouth, and if there is any unforeseen hitch I shall swallow it."

"That won't help much if McLean suspects you. But there is no reason why he should suspect if you work quickly. Once you reach the car you are safe. Nothing is likely to overtake Pat. We are going to get the thing this time. Why, I've already sold it!"

Dolly laughed admiringly.

"You're a nut, Amos," she said. "What's it worth to us?"

"Twenty thousand."

"Lordy! I hope nothing goes wrong. I need some more glad rags and a change of climate."

"You'll get them," replied Feeny.

A week passed, and at nine o'clock in the evening Feeny sat in his flat, with a big Alsatian dog sprawling at his feet. He was agitated and kept glancing at the clock on the mantelpiece. There came a ring at the bell, and he answered it himself, for the maid had purposely been sent on an errand. Dolly entered, and looked at him inquiringly.

"No news yet," he said.

"Isn't it rather late?"

"A bit later than I expected, but Streeter won't fail. He's to get two thousand out of this, and is pretty well stone broke. He's clever too."

She reclined in a chair, helped herself to a whisky-and-soda, and patted the dog.

"Happy days for us, Wolf, if we get away with this," she mused. "Have a biccy?"

The dog became more alert, and swallowed the biscuit whole.

"Why, he's starving!" she complained. "Why don't you feed him?"

"He's all right. Always hungry. Gosh, I wish Streeter would turn up. Nearly a quarter-past the hour!"

Time passed and their nerves got on edge. It was half-past nine when they heard the sound of running feet. Feeny sprang up and rushed to the front door. As he opened it Streeter almost fell through it.

"Well?"

"I've got it, but McLean is on my heels."

"What!"

"I leapt out of the car at Greek Street, and Pat

went off to the garage. Cut through the park to force McLean's car to stop. He—he came after me."

"Damn him! But where's the stone—quick?"

"Here."

Streeter produced a magnificent ruby. Feeny's eyes blazed as he saw it. It was mounted on a stout gold pin and was the finest thing he had ever set eyes on.

"Plant it—somewhere," gasped Streeter.

"Do you think McLean saw you enter here?"

"I don't know. What's that?"

It was a long ring at the bell. Feeny started, and looked round for a hiding-place. Streeter and the woman grew nervous. The dog stretched himself. It gave Feeny an idea. He ran out to the larder and came back with a hunk of meat. Into this he pressed the ruby and then offered it to Wolf. The hungry dog gave one short sniff, and meat and jewel disappeared in a gulp.

"Kennel!" ordered Feeny, and opened the casement window. The obedient dog went off at once. Again and again the bell rang.

"I'll go," said Feeny. "Got your breath? Good. Remember you have been here all evening. Spread out that pack of cards—quick!"

At the door was McLean. He knew Feeny quite well, and Feeny knew him.

"Hullo, Inspector!" said Feeny coolly. "What's all this noise?"

"I've just come to have a look at you, Feeny," said McLean calmly. "Any objection?"

"None. As a matter of fact you can make a fourth in a game of bridge. We are only three."

"That's a pity. But I daresay the driver of your car will be back soon. He seemed to be in a hurry to garage it. Fast little vehicle that! I had quite a job to keep in touch with it."

"You will have your little joke, McLean," laughed Feeny. "But I am such a stickler for conventions that I do not play cards with my chauffeur, who at this moment is probably in bed. But come right in."

McLean entered the sitting-room, where Streeter and Dolly were talking. They had been quick to act, and the cards were dealt in four lots. Close by were scoring blocks with figures on them. McLean smiled.

"No need for introductions," he said. "The lady and I have met three times before, and Mr. Streeter here served me with an excellent brand of port this evening."

Streeter looked at McLean with well-simulated amazement.

"I don't quite follow that," he said.

"Your memory is extraordinarily short. But you should have changed your boots. There is a small amount of gravel still adhering to them from the Duke's newly-made path."

"Duke?" said Streeter. "What on earth are

you talking about? And you certainly have the advantage of me."

McLean had done with banter. His expression became grim and he advanced on Streeter.

"Wise men snatch at opportunities," he said. "I am going to give you all a chance. This evening you, Streeter—oh yes, I know your name—you got away with a valuable jewel. You brought it here less than ten minutes ago. Hand it over and I'll leave you in peace. I make this concession because its real owner wishes to leave England to-morrow, and naturally wants to take his property with him. Come along."

"You are making a mistake," said Streeter. "I have been in this house for over two hours. Feeny and Doll can swear to it."

"You refuse a very generous offer?"

"It may seem generous to you, but it doesn't to me."

"Will you hand over that jewel?"

"I'm sorry—I can't, for reasons that should be obvious."

"Then I must find it—and finding it means a pretty long stretch for you."

Feeny walked up and down, simulating anger.

"Can't sit down to a game of cards without the police rushing in and making wild accusations——!"

"Shut up!" snapped McLean. "I'll take you in turn. I've got a man outside, so I advise you to be docile."

"Let him have his way," said Feeny. "I suppose you want to go through my pockets?"

"I do. I'll take you first."

This to Streeter, who promptly stood up and raised his hands above his head. McLean's nimble fingers went everywhere, and at last he was satisfied that Streeter no longer possessed the ruby. Feeny then submitted to being searched, and the result was the same. Dolly then came forward.

"Oh, Inspector," she cooed. "This is most embarrassing. I hope you're a married man?"

"I rather hope you're a married woman," retorted McLean dryly.

"Here, what do you mean by that?"

"A veiled compliment. Stand still!"

He had, more or less, to give her the benefit of the doubt, but he now felt moderately certain that the jewel was "planted," and probably planted well. In the meantime his chauffeur had telephoned Scotland Yard, and while he was busy ransacking the sitting-room, Sergeant Brook and two helpers arrived.

"I'm looking for a jewel," he said. "A big ruby. It is in this house. Brook, you can take charge of these persons. You other two can help me. Up with that carpet!"

For two solid hours the search went on, until there remained no single inch of the flat that had not been examined. McLean had to abandon the search at last. He had good grounds for arresting Streeter, but he preferred not to at this juncture.

"Satisfied?" asked Feeny.

"I'm satisfied that you have hidden it rather well. But you haven't got away with it yet, Feeny, and you were foolish not to accept my offer. I am sorry it cannot be repeated."

Feeny laughed, and intimated that he would like to go to bed at some time or other. Streeter looked a trifle anxious, but sighed when he heard McLean tell his assistants that he had finished for that night. The police went, but the trio stayed together for some time, discussing the immediate future.

§

But McLean had no intention of abandoning the matter at that juncture. It was obvious that the ruby was either in the house or in the car in which Streeter had escaped, but he favoured the house, because it offered better chance of concealment. The man who had driven the car had vanished, but McLean believed he would join his confederates when he believed the coast was clear. So he dismissed his assistants with the exception of Brook.

"I expect that chauffeur to call later," he said. "If so we will nab him, and endeavour to locate the car."

They took up a position in the park which permitted them to observe the house without being seen. Neither Dolly nor Streeter emerged, but some time later McLean saw a curtain pulled aside and a vague form appear behind it.

"Watching," he said. "I fancy they will leave the house before morning."

Half an hour later a form approached the house. McLean was convinced it was the chauffeur, though it was impossible to identify him. He whispered instructions to Brook and the pair cut off the man's approach.

"Where are you going?" demanded McLean.

"Home," replied Dugan.

McLean flashed the torch in his face and recognised him as an old lag.

"Pat Dugan!" he said. "So it was you. I want to know what you have done with that car."

"What car?"

"No nonsense. I'll take you right along now unless you talk up. You brought Streeter to the other side of the park and dropped him, while you garaged the car. Where is it?"

"I tell you——"

"Handcuff him!" ordered McLean. "If he insists upon doing a stretch, that's his business."

Brook produced a pair of handcuffs, but Pat waved him aside.

"Wait!" he begged. "Inspector, do you mean you'll leave me out of this if I take you to the car?"

"Yes—provided I satisfy myself you haven't got the ruby."

"All right. I'll take you to the car."

"You go, Brook," said McLean. "Watch him carefully. Better slip the bracelets on, but you can let him go when you are satisfied he hasn't got the jewel. Search that car, and then come back here. I want to keep an eye on our friends."

Pat was handcuffed, and he and Brook went off. About ten minutes later a car drew up at Feeny's house. It was a hired vehicle, and McLean guessed it had been telephoned for—when Dugan failed to arrive. The driver rang the bell, and Feeny answered it. A few minutes later Feeny, Streeter and Dolly left the house, accompanied by the dog, and entered the car. McLean just had time to leave the park and mount the luggage grid of the car ere it started off. It went at a great pace through many deserted streets and into the country beyond Wimbledon. Ultimately it pulled up outside the drive of an old isolated house. Fortunately there was a large elm tree at the rear of the car and McLean was able to take shelter behind it. The driver was paid off—handsomely to judge from his profuse thanks—and the trio and the dog walked up the drive. McLean saw them enter the house. He stopped the chauffeur of the car just as he was about to start away.

"I am a police officer, and I want you to take me back to the house from which you brought those people."

"A police officer!"

"There's no time for explanations. Drive as fast as you can."

He was whirled back to the spot where he had promised to meet Brook, and found his subordinate there, mystified by his disappearance.

"I had to leave," he explained. "What about the car?"

"Nothing hidden there, I'll swear. I went through that fellow's pockets. He hasn't got the ruby."

"I guessed not. The other crowd left with a dog. I didn't know there was a dog. Did you search his kennel?"

"I was looking after Feeny," replied Brook. "You told me to."

"So I did. I'll bet Samuels missed the kennel. He is scared to death of dogs. But it's useless now. If it was there they will have removed it. We had better get to Wimbledon. If once we lose touch with Feeny—good-bye to the Rajah's ruby. He is as clever as a cartload of monkeys."

The chauffeur seemed to be a little tired of nocturnal trips, but he did as he was ordered, and in a very short time McLean and Brook were outside the lonely house.

" Can I go now ? " begged the chauffeur.

" I'm afraid not. Why worry ? Look at the money you are earning ! "

" I've been up since six this morning."

" You can sleep all day to-morrow. Wait here. Your next trip may be to Scotland Yard. We shall see."

" Are we going to enter ? " asked Brook.

" Yes. This time we may be more fortunate."

There was a light burning in the front downstairs room, but McLean had no intention of giving the thieves warning of his approach. He and Brook entered the house through a basement window, and moved cautiously up the stairs towards the hall. On reaching the room in which the light was burning the door was pushed open suddenly, and the two men entered. The woman—Dolly—was sitting before a gas-fire in a kimono patting the big Alsatian dog, who looked very miserable. He did not even growl at the intruders. Dolly gasped.

" You ! Again ! "

" Where's Feeny ? "

" Gone."

" Where ? "

" I don't know."

" You do know."

" I tell you I don't. He went off with Streeter."

"Why did you leave that other house in a hurry?"

"This is my house, and I wanted to get home."

"And they both accompanied you like the gallant gentlemen they are?"

"Yes."

"And is this your dog?"

"Yes. Feeny was looking after him for me."

"He looks sick."

"He is not very well."

"You refuse to tell me where those two men have gone?"

"I tell you I don't know."

"And you don't know where the ruby is?"

"No."

"Then I do."

She stared at him.

"We made rather a blunder at the other place. We overlooked the dog. That was Feeny's idea, wasn't it?"

"I don't know what you mean."

"You soon will. I know for a positive fact that Streeter took that jewel to the other house. There was only one possible hiding-place that we overlooked. I am going to prove my theory now."

He drew his pistol and bade Dolly stand aside.

"What—what are you going to do?" she gasped.

"The ruby was given to the dog, wrapped up in a hunk of meat. I am going to——"

With a cry of horror she leapt at him and seized his wrist. Brook compressed his lips, not yet fully appreciating McLean's motive.

"Hold her!" snapped McLean. "The dog has it—hence his sickness. It was a big stone——"

"Stop!" screamed Dolly. "You can't shoot my dog. It isn't true—at least——"

"It will be painless——"

"No—no. He hasn't got it. Feeny gave it to him, but we brought him here to get it back. Feeny gave him a strong emetic, and succeeded in——"

"I'm not taking any chances," interrupted McLean. "Hold her, Brook."

He raised the pistol and held it close to the dog's heart. Dolly struggled wildly and gasped.

"Stop! I swear Feeny has the ruby. Pat Dugan came here in the car—soon after we arrived. He told us he had been apprehended, but that he had been let go. They all went off—to Southampton—to catch a boat in the morning. Feeny wouldn't take me, but he paid me some money—look!"

She put out her hand and seized her handbag, then produced a wad of notes. McLean put away his pistol. At last she had spoken the truth.

"When did they leave?" he demanded

"Half an hour ago."

He wasted no more time with Dolly. The great thing was to overtake Dugan's fast car, and with half an hour's start that seemed almost an impossible task. They ran from the house and told the chauffeur what was required of him. But that worthy refused to go. He was dog-tired and wasn't fit to drive.

"Then we'll tåke the car," said McLean. "You must find your way home somehow. Police will be responsible. How is the petrol?"

"Nearly a full tank."

"Good! Take the wheel, Brook, and let her rip. I'll direct you to the main road."

§

McLean soon wished he had not let the police car go back to headquarters, but it would have wasted valuable time to get it again, and he had to make the most of the hired vehicle. Fortunately it was a high-powered car and capable of quite fair speed. Brook was an excellent driver and they were soon well into the country. Along the main road Brook trod hard on the accelerator pedal and the car responded well. But in spite of reckless speed, over sixty miles were covered without their seeing a sign of Dugan's car.

"We've got to get them within the next

half-hour," said McLean. "Won't she do any more?"

"Not an ounce. Phew—that was a narrow squeak!"

This as a sudden bend was taken and the back of the car skidded frightfully. Five minutes later a red light was seen in the distance.

"That may be him," said McLean. "Hang on!"

Brook did hang on. He took bends and corners at a rate that should have spelt suicide, but always he managed to get the car right after hair-breadth skids. At times the red light seemed to be nearer, and every few minutes it vanished round bends. Then it became apparent that the car ahead was Dugan's car, and that its occupants had awakened to the fact that they were being pursued. On the straight sections of road the distance between them increased, but on the bends Brook held his own.

"They've got to stop somewhere," said Brook. "And when they do we'll get them."

But he had scarcely spoken the words when the car swerved almost into the hedge. The steering seemed to have gone wrong, and pace was immediately reduced.

"That's done it!" grunted Brook. "Front wheel puncture! We'll lose them now."

McLean bit his lip. The road ahead was perfectly straight for at least a mile. He saw the fugitive car moving away, and then the headlights of it illuminated a level crossing. McLean's heart leapt with joy, for the bar was coming down. The fugitives realised it too, and the low fast car literally swept across the intervening space. It passed under the first bar, but failed to clear the second. The bonnet hit the obstruction and snapped it off like a carrot, but the impact wrenched the wheel from the driver's hands. The car swerved, rushed madly up a steep bank, hit a tree and then turned completely over.

The noise brought the night porter rushing to the scene, and McLean and Brook arrived a few seconds later on their flat tyre. McLean leapt out and went to the scene of the catastrophe. Dugan was wedged beside the driving wheel, with both arms broken, and in the rear of the vehicle Streeter and Feeny were lying in a welter of blood caused by the broken glass. They had to be got out through the windows, and it was soon apparent that Streeter was doomed, for his neck was shockingly lacerated. Feeny's injuries were less severe.

" Send for a doctor," said McLean to the porter.

When the man departed he turned his attention to Feeny, who was quite conscious but very weak.

" Better hand it over, Feeny. It's all up."

" You're wrong," snarled Feeny. " We've got nothing."

" It's here in the car."

" Find it then."

" Inspector," said Brook. " This fellow is through."

McLean turned to Streeter, who had now regained consciousness, and was trying to speak.

" You are trying to tell me where the ruby is ? "

Streeter's head moved slightly, also his lips, but no sound came. It was clear he had but a few minutes to live.

" Is it in the car ? " asked McLean.

The head indicated that it was.

" Under cushions ? "

The head said " no."

" Tool-bag—lamps—tank—in a tool——? "

He was stopped by a movement of the head, then suddenly Streeter shuddered and his head drooped.

" He's gone," said Brook. " Poor devil ! He tried to tell us. It's in a tool, but what tool ? "

" Have a look at the driver," said McLean. " He's in pain. I'll rout out all the tools."

He managed to open one of the doors, and then collected all the tools together. Feeny watched him from where he lay, and his eyes glowed with hate as McLean pulled everything to pieces. At last the grease-gun was taken up. Feeny's eyes divulged the secret. Within a few seconds the cap was screwed off, and McLean was hunting in the thick grease. His fingers touched a hard object, and a screw-driver secured its removal. It was the Rajah's ruby!

" At last ! " said McLean. " So you planned to get the car across the Channel too ? "

" Yes," snapped Feeny. " I suppose that girl gave us away ? I thought she was reliable. Women spoil everything."

" She has a saving grace," said McLean. " She is deeply attached to her dog."

THE END